D0016460

The Vespertine

The Vespertine

SAUNDRA MITCHELL

YOLO COUNTY LIBRARY
226 BUCKEYE STREET
WOODLAND CA 95695

HARCOURT

Houghton Mifflin Harcourt

Boston   New York   2011

Copyright © 2011 by Saundra Mitchell

All rights reserved. For information about permission to reproduce selections from this book, write to Permissions, Houghton Mifflin Harcourt Publishing Company, 215 Park Avenue South, New York, New York 10003.

Harcourt is an imprint of Houghton Mifflin Harcourt Publishing Company.

www.hmhbooks.com

Text set in Cochin
Design by Regina Roff

Library of Congress Cataloging-in-Publication Data is available.

Manufactured in the United States of America
DOC 10 9 8 7 6 5 4 3 2 1
4500276210

For Nick and Gwen—
There are more things . . .

✳

Oakhaven

Broken Tooth, Maine

Autumn 1889

✳

One

I WOKE IN OAKHAVEN, entirely ruined.

The ballad notes of a quadrille lingered on my skin, remnants of a *chaîne anglaise* danced only in slumber. I heard a velvet voice against my cheek, and I burned in the dark and dreaming light of his eyes.

Morning had come, its watery brightness stealing shadows from the corners, but still I swayed.

Perhaps this once I could find my visions—my awful, eerie gift—without the fires of sunset. Perhaps this once I could abandon the vespers and go there on my own. To the place where I saw more than eyes could see. Where I knew more than minds could know.

Where I could be with him.

I had learned to do it for Zora, my sweetest friend—lost, and I was to blame! I couldn't bear to wonder about her. I knew how I'd left her—wrecked and desolate, a shell because I'd cracked her open. I should have listened when she told me to bear it alone.

If some ethereal part of me counted sins, that part bore the darkest stain for the tragedy I brought her. Rocking until the floor kept time, I drew a breath elongated. I opened my arms to open my body.

If I could spill everything out, if I could but empty myself of sensation and thought, I could be filled again with the sight. If this were sunset, the visions would come. Through my mind's eye, I would step inside someone else's skin.

I'd walk on their legs, see with their eyes—whispers of all things to come. Until now I'd been too afraid to look for my older, wiser self. Today I whispered and rocked, and rolled my eyes, hoping to see anything at all.

The need overwhelmed me, my breath rushing like wind, blood pounding in my ears—all distractions, terrible distractions. I begged through bitten lips, "Please, please, please . . ."

My skirts washed around me. I made fists of my hands, nails digging into the palms. If only pain brought clarity!

Locked in this hopeless attic room, I flung myself at the desk. How viciously darling of my brother. He'd jailed me with pen and paper, but no one to write to.

I had nothing. I had no one.

Weighted by the ornate train of my gown, I climbed up. Only on my toes could I see the world outside, the first peach and plum shades of morning in the distance. Something heavy in me turned. I flattened my hands on the glass.

"Nathaniel, Nathaniel!" I cried, then seized by a terrible rage, I screamed. "How could you abandon me to this?"

I beat at the windows. I imagined my fists shattering the panes, shards making ribbons of my flesh. I tasted the blood. I felt the cold that would come of letting it course from me. This was no premonition, just dread hope.

Intention weighed my arms. I stood coiled. I meant to spring! To have it done! To end it all!

But my craven nature restrained me. The threat of pain made me a coward. I could only slap the glass uselessly. Ashamed, I pressed my brow against the wall and wept.

Then the attic door swung open.

Startled, I lost my balance entirely. The desk tipped over, and my skirts dragged me down like an anchor. In a shower of writing paper and unstoppered bottles, I fell to the floor.

India ink splashed in black puddles, and my hands came up smeared with it.

August, my pale and angled brother, hauled me to my feet. His fingers bit through my sleeves, writing five hot points of pain on my flesh.

"What's the matter with you?" he demanded.

"Nothing at all! I am fit and bright and sober as a priest."

With another shake, August asked, "Shall I send you to the sanitarium after all?"

"You should!" I shouted.

"Don't test me, Amelia," August said, his voice rising. "I will beat the devil out of you. You have my word on that."

I couldn't help but smile. "You can't. You'd have to beat me dead. What will you do with your devil sister's body, Gus? How will you explain me away?"

He answered me with a slap. It left a welt on my cheek, raised and burning, and all I could do was touch it gingerly — and laugh. Softly, but laughter all the same, for August was far more troubled by it than I.

Gray as wash water, he cast an accusing look at his hand.

I lay back, turning my eyes to the plastered ceiling to welcome a weary numbness. "Just poison my breakfast. You can call it a fever. Be done with me," I told him as I dropped to the bed.

"I doted on you once." Backing toward the door, August looked everywhere but at me. "I used to pull you about in my wagon."

"I'm much too heavy for your wagon now."

Taking out his key, August warned me as he once more locked me in, "Stay away from the windows."

Perhaps tomorrow, I thought, *I shall be brave enough to put myself through them.*

✻ ✻ ✻

Clattering footsteps came up the stairs, carried with the sounds of an argument well and truly started.

". . . cannot simply lock her away, August!"

"She is ruined. I do think I can . . ."

". . . sent her to make friends and find a husband, you can hardly complain that she tried in earnest . . ."

Flattening myself against the door, I pressed my ear to it to listen. Strange hope battered my chest. August's tender-hearted wife intended to set me free. Loose in the house, I could devise a hundred methods to dispatch myself, ones painless enough to conquer my cowardice.

"Enough!" Lizzy stamped a foot, and I felt the floor vibrate with it.

Rushing back to the bed, I fixed my eyes on the ink-stained floor. My heart fluttered with shame. Here came a little brown bird of a girl, pleasantly ordinary in every way, to my defense without knowing the sort of chaos I could cause.

They whispered a moment more, and then the key ground in the lock. When the door swung open, Lizzy opened her arms to me.

"Amelia Grace," she said. "Welcome home."

We had always been cordial but never fond. This once, Lizzy embraced me tenderly.

"I am glad to come to it," I murmured.

Lizzy folded her hands serenely and turned to August. "Shall we to breakfast? Jennie's still away, but can't we cobble something together?"

My stomach twisted, and I marveled at my body's will against my mind. These hands would not break glass; this belly would not go hungry. Perhaps the truth was that I was weak and simple-minded, easy to beguile. I wondered if that meant all my feelings were false. Would every passion I'd known fade away with time and sensibility?

Finally, I said, "I believe we can."

"Splendid," Lizzy said. She put a hand on August's arm, steering him with a great deal more subtlety than he had steered me the night before. "While we meddle in the kitchen, could you see to it that Amelia's room near mine is put right?"

Oh, I could see the refusal on August's tongue; he stuck it out, just the tip, then bit down to end his inward struggle. Forcing a smile, he offered me a slanted look. "Of course, dear wife."

"I should change," I said. Ink stained my gown and my hands. My hair hung in lank, weedy stripes over my shoulders.

"We're all family here." Lizzy smiled pleasantly, first at me, then at August.

Without speaking to me, without even once straying toward a glance, August took his leave.

❀ ❀ ❀

Lizzy considered a knotty loaf of bread, touching the knife to it several times before deciding where to cut. I waited quietly beside her, playing with the cage on the long-handled bread toaster.

"One for the bag," she said, tossing the heel into a muslin bag set aside for bread pudding. Then she made two more cuts and offered me thick, even slices on the flat of her knife. "And two for you."

Perched on a little stool, I turned the toaster in my hands. My face stung with the heat rolling out, the flames drawing a fine sheen of sweat to my face.

Still slicing, Lizzy swayed, the satin of her tea gown whispering with the motion. There was a great deal to be said for keeping a tidy appearance. Though Lizzy's curls were unremarkably dun and her features simply regular, she had a delicate air.

None would handle her roughly nor pull the pins from her hair. Certainly none would leave ragged the edges of her Irish lace. She wore respectability like earbobs, a subtle touch noticed by all who knew her.

I spun the toaster's handle again and tried to find my voice. "You're good to have me downstairs."

"You're family."

"It would please August if I weren't," I said. It was shockingly wrong to hint at the reason for my return, and yet how could I not? "I never intended . . ."

Softly, Lizzy said, "I believe you're making charcoal."

Jerking the toaster from the stove, I shook it to put out the flames. "I'm sorry!"

I scrambled for a cloth to wrap around my hand and yet managed to burn myself all the same. When I went to apologize again, nothing came out but a plaintive sob, and suddenly I found myself cosseted in Lizzy's arms again.

"You should know," she said, patting my back in a matter-of-fact kind of way, "that there's still life left in a ruined girl."

"You're kind," I said, and mostly meant it. "But it's not so. I intended to be good, Lizzy. I meant to make myself a good match and a wholesome friend, but . . ."

"But what?" she asked.

I lifted my face to her, brokenly certain. "But now I'm not fit for anything but haunting my brother's house."

"You'd make a fine lady clerk or teacher," Lizzy said. She took a step back, squaring me with her hands on my shoulders. "If that's what you'd choose. But believe me when I tell you, little sister. Time rubs away most stains, and it is with utmost certainty that I assure you . . ."

For a long moment, she said nothing. Then her voice went low as she confided, "There are good men who won't care that the package is dented, should its contents delight them."

Did she mean she'd been . . . I took a breath when she nodded, confirming it. I should've been shocked to find out Lizzy had ever sinned, let alone sinned so much as to ruin her. I should have been shocked, but I wasn't. Instead, numbness soothed me, a balm for my ragged heart that still yearned for a monster.

Squeezing Lizzy's hand, I swore, "It would be a wasted soul to find you anything but delightful."

"Well then," Lizzy said brightly. "Shall we attempt our toast and jam again?"

❋

Kestrels

Baltimore, Maryland

Spring 1889

❋

Two

U NLIKE THE SEEMLY, segregated docks in New York City, Baltimore's northwest harbor was a fantastic place to step into an adventure.

Though my cousin Mrs. Stewart did her utmost to keep me from oggling at the sailors and shoremen, only a hood would have hidden them from me completely.

What marvels they were, some fine in uniforms from the best and worst steam lines, a Cunarder cap there, and the crisp, familiar white and red of the White Star Line on down the way. But the coal men and crabbers I found the most fascinating, for I had landed in Maryland on an unseasonably warm day.

My blouse clung to my flesh in those rare places my corset didn't confine, but these men all adock had no such troubles. Half of them had stripped to the skin, muslin shirts hanging from their belts, suspenders crossing bared chests and broad shoulders.

"Move along," Mrs. Stewart said, herding me with her parasol against my bustle. In spite of her hurry, I gazed my fill.

Young men, thin as whippets, ranged before us. They tipped hats and called hello in a way that said they *knew* they had no business greeting ladies this way. Some had accents, melodious hints of countries I'd read about but never seen. Others spoke with the same down-home tones Mrs. Stewart did.

"Out of the way," she threatened when one blue-eyed tease of a lad, this one at least fully dressed and no more than ten, fell into step beside us.

"It's trouble on the docks for ladies alone," he said, pulling his hat off and pressing it to his chest. He implored me, as if I had any say in the matter of my direction. "Beg you let me see your way to your carriage."

"We have not one penny for you, young man. Good day."

Mrs. Stewart not only led visiting cousins by the rod of her parasol, but she drove off churls with it, too. She threatened with its lace and silk, and the boy melted into the crowd again. When he did, Mrs. Stewart made a triumphant sound, then looked to me.

"Have no doubt of it, Miss van den Broek, Baltimore is everything brash and forward." She hooked my elbow and steered me neatly around a broken board. "We'll make you a good match yet, but we won't find it here—mind your step."

"Fair enough," I said softly, laughing when a fruit vendor, an Araber, tossed up a pale green trio of apples to juggle.

A single yearning "Oh" escaped my lips.

My trip from Broken Tooth to Baltimore had lasted barely three days, but it had left me oversalted and undersweetened. The perfume from those apples burned my nose, sharpening my appetite with raw hunger.

I had no pocket money of my own. The price for keeping me was folded in a thick leather folio, tucked safely in Mrs. Stewart's coat. There was enough for a few gowns and necessaries. I'd need those to make proper friendships, hopefully a marriageable match, this summer—there was nothing more necessary than that, as far as my brother was concerned. Apples, however tempting, could hardly be considered so important.

Mrs. Stewart glanced at me, then traded a coin for an apple before hurrying me into the cobbled brick street. "Save it 'til we're on the road," she said.

Of course, I wouldn't thwart her; I clung to my apple and followed gratefully, until we came to a roundabout and an unattended victoria.

Though the leather seats shone a bit, worn in places from use, it was a glorious little car. The bonnet top was folded back, its wheel spokes painted gaily red—this carriage was worlds more delightful than the funereal rockaway carriage August kept at home.

Mrs. Stewart put her foot in one of the front spokes, looking over her shoulder at me. "In you go."

A flutter filled my chest, watching her hitch her skirts daintily and climb into the driver's seat. Trailing my gloved hand along the hitched horse's flank, I asked, "You'll be driving, ma'am?"

"We're no relation to the Commodore," she said, and of course intended to remind me that though I was a *van*, mine was *den Broek* and not *der Bilt*. "I'll drive or we'll swelter all day here. If it's all the same to you, I'd prefer suffocating at home."

"Where *is* Mr. Stewart?" I inquired, still lingering.

With brisk, gloved hands at the reins, Mrs. Stewart looked down at me. "At his office, I expect. The law's as much a calling as the cloth."

"I see," I said.

"Come on now. Lizzy told me you weren't the precious sort. Even if you are, I'm the driver you've got."

Chastened, I blushed and moved to climb in the carriage. But at once, I stopped.

I'm not entirely sure what possessed me. Maybe the loneliness of the cab, or the novelty of a lady driver, or just the wild air of the Inner Harbor in my lungs, but I asked, "Is there room up front, Mrs. Stewart?"

Mrs. Stewart answered my question with a distinct slide to the right. I folded my skirts as I'd seen her do and stepped up. From this perch, I could see the whole of Baltimore—it was a magnificent view.

"Have that apple now," Mrs. Stewart said, seamlessly urging the horse into traffic. "Caesar here will want the core."

My teeth cut into the fruit's firm and fragrant skin, and I tasted something entirely new as Mrs. Stewart drove us away from the harbor side.

Narrow row houses shone with white marble steps; the streets swelled with splashes of color—riotous silk gowns and cheerful vests cut in shades of earth and grass and sky. Children darted in front of our wheels, but miraculously survived their own derring-do, girls and boys alike. So many songs slipped into my ears—the call of Arabers, the shouts of newspaper boys, and delightfully, oddly, someone playing a pianoforte.

Somehow this struck me all as a daydream, a mythological fantasia too great to be real. All my life I'd lived on our cliff, looking down on a fishing village so small, I could raise my thumb to cover it. A season in town had been beyond my imagination. This great chaos and cry, smelling of sea and smoke and open ground—*this* was a *city*. My heart beat with it. My thoughts roared with it!

With another crisp bite of apple, I tasted—perhaps for the first time—the true sweetness of possibility.

❋ ❋ ❋

"We'll share this bed. And I've cleared half the armoire for your things."

Clad in cherry silk, Zora Stewart moved as if her feet never touched the floor. She had a high color in her cheeks, her heart-shaped face delicate as a bisque doll's.

Curls escaped the sweep of her dark hair, coppery coils that served only to draw her throat longer and more elegant still. Only the faintest spray of freckles across her nose gave hint that she was anything but perfection.

"It's good of you to have me." I bowed my head, an imitation of her serene air that felt so unfamiliar, it could have been mockery. Lizzy was right. I'd spent too many years rusticating in the Down East, reading about manners but never truly practicing them.

"It wasn't as though I had a choice." Lights danced in Zora's eyes, hinting at the nimble mind wrapped in such a lovely package of grace and femininity. She had not spoken crossly. In fact, amusement touched the edge of her lips. "Can you polish boots?"

I played along. "I can, and darn socks and rebone stays . . ."

"How are you, I wonder," she said, as she turned to open the window, "at making biscuits?"

I covered my heart with my hand and confessed, "A failure, I admit. I'm told my biscuits suit nicely when there are no rocks to be had for a slingshot."

A soft breath of wind flooded into the room, stirring trapped heat and urging it away. Zora leaned against the windowsill and smiled. "Brilliant. I'm forever running short of ammunition for my slingshot."

"I have never been away from home," I told her.

"I have never had a friend to stay," she replied.

At once, we both took an accounting. Her gown was more fashionable; my hair more intricately dressed. In stillness, she held her hands with grace, and I sprawled, ungainly along the edge of the bed. In that moment, I suppose we could have decided to be rivals.

Instead, Zora took my hand and said, "We're too grand to stay indoors today, I believe."

❀ ❀ ❀

Twining down streets that spread in a chaotic burst from Druid Hill Park, we took in sunshine and our fill of sightseeing — or, rather, sightseeing for me and sight-showing for her.

"Four mornings a week," Zora told me, tugging at a locked door, "we'll come here for classes. You won't care much for Miss Burnside."

Lifting my skirts, I rose to peer in the window. It looked like any private home on the block, though a plate by the door read SWANN DAY SCHOOL.

"I only had a tutor."

Zora nodded. "My friends Sarah and Mattie share a tutor, but Papa is fascinated with progress. Co-educational learning! Gaslight on tap! You should see the way he trembles in excitement when he talks about the new train line going in. Chicago's the future, he claims. We need a direct route to it!"

"August isn't modern at all," I said. "He's quite old-fashioned, in fact. He would have married me off by now if there were anyone in Broken Tooth *to* marry."

Wrinkling her nose, Zora asked, "What sort of name is Broken Tooth?"

"An accurate one," I said.

It was a hard-working village, small and spare. We had no regular doctor; dentistry was done in the barbershop. I supposed it made August feel like a lord to live on a hill above it all. Down East he could pretend to be a society man. I didn't bother explaining that, though. We Van den Broeks shared that pride, it seemed—I didn't want Zora to think I was more backward than she already must.

With a winning smile, I changed the subject. "So I'm looking forward to going to school with you!"

Zora looped her arm through mine to drag me away. "I already earned the first desk. It drives the boys to distraction.

Have you taken Latin or Greek? You'll have to start at the last, but if you unseated them your first week . . . oh!"

Bewildered, I asked, "Unseat them how?"

"With lessons. The first of the class earn the desks closest to the front; the last are sadly relegated to the shadows in back. It's farthest from the stove and the lamps and the windows."

"Sounds miserable," I said.

And to my delight, Zora laughed, a soft, naughty sound. "It is."

"Secretly, you're a beast, aren't you?"

"There will be time enough for sainthood once I'm married," she said.

Then, with a strength I never would have thought possible, she yanked my arm, pulling me down an alley. Our forcible departure from the road startled me, my thoughts unsettled by a strange, sharp scent I couldn't place. There was no gate nor welcome to invite us through this passage, but Zora walked it with sturdy familiarity.

Pausing, Zora pressed a finger to her lips. Then she gathered her skirts so they would do no whispering as we crept into a set of adjoined yards. White wooden fences separated them, fist-size spaces between each plank giving us much room to peek through.

The high note of a struck axe rose up. I noted first the blade, dull at the handle and bright at the edge, catching sunlight and tossing it with a flash. His hair caught some of that spark, a little long and falling loose, brushing past eyes certainly light in shade. I was too far to make out the color exactly.

I ascertained that should I truly wish to know, I'd only have to ask Zora, whose grip tightened uncomfortably on my elbow.

"Thomas Rea," she said. She kept her voice low as she pulled me along the fences, for it seemed we needed to look on Thomas at many angles. "His father's a bachelor or a widower. It's our little mystery trying to guess which."

Oblivious to us, Thomas split through his lot of wood, oddly graceful at it. Such a brute chore should have been ugly to watch. Instead, it was a wonder, the way he turned a pile of maple into an orderly cord for burning.

"He's almost in our circle." Zora put her hands on my shoulders, ducking around me to get a better view. "Since his father's a doctor, that's respectable enough. But no one knows them, really. Sarah's mother is beside herself, trying to decide if any of us can marry Thomas."

I covered my mouth to hide my smile. "Is that so?"

"Mrs. Holbrook plots. It's her opium." Suddenly, Zora crumpled against the fence.

Hurrying to attend her, I asked, "Are you faint?"

"Simply mad, Amelia."

Zora exhaled a sigh, looking through the slats again. Her lashes fluttered as she battled her stays for a deep breath. Her hands had turned to hard knots, held tight at her waist. Deliberately, she brushed herself off and headed for the alley.

Though I mainly played at my charcoals, I had a moment of inspiration. Zora would make such an ideal Thisbe! How entirely like her in that moment, longing for a Pyramus at work with his axe. I imagined sketching holly in her hair and wispy gowns flowing from her shoulders . . .

"You're dawdling. Don't you want to get to the printer's today?"

Protesting, I swore, "I don't think August intended my allowance to be spent on calling cards!"

"Dash August, then," Zora said. "We'll spend it anyway!"

Newly dizzy with daring, I held up one finger. "A moment, wait!" And in my madness, fed by hers, I stepped up on the fence and called out, "Fancy you, Thomas, good afternoon!"

"Amelia!" Zora cried, her delight both complete and horrified.

I never knew if Thomas raised his head to see us, for Zora ran away laughing. What could I do but run after her?

Three

"THAT'S A MAN'S CARD," Zora said, tugging a catalog from my hands. "What's the matter with you?"

"I like them!"

Reaching for the printer's book, I longed to look at the handsome calling card again, the one with a silhouette of a hawk. It seemed all the cards I preferred were meant for men—the ones with bold strokes and dark letters.

Nostrils flaring, Zora presented me with one of her cards. "See, there. That's a proper lady's card. Ivory and silver and script. Don't you think it introduces me well?"

"It's very like you," I agreed, rubbing the ivory edges of it. "But I . . ."

"That's the living end, Charles," Mrs. Stewart shouted from downstairs.

Zora's eyes went wide, and I felt my pulse tick up. That could only be Mr. Stewart, and what could be so devastating as to make my most proper cousin shout like a fishwife? Zora dumped cards and catalog alike on the bed and motioned for me to follow her to the stairs.

We tried not to clatter, keeping our shoes firmly on the blue carpeting. When the wall gave way to open banister, we crouched to listen.

"Ohhhhh," Zora said, resting her hand on my neck. "James Keller canceled on us again. Listen to Mama rant."

"Honestly, are we made of money? That boy's naught but a useless rag!"

Mr. Stewart laughed, then shut up immediately. "I'm sorry, dear heart."

When all went silent, Zora and I exchanged a look. Like fire jumping from the hearth, we both leaped up. A fine, tall man ruined our escape when he appeared at the bottom of the stairs. Zora resembled him most remarkably.

"You must be our boarder," he said, with the same smile that Zora'd used when she asked if I could polish boots. He turned an expectant look on his daughter as he put on his hat.

Zora skimmed down the stairs—the same vision of

unearthly beauty I had met that morning. She leaned toward her father and reached back for me at once. "Papa, may I present Amelia van den Broek? Amelia, this is my father, Mr. Stewart."

I tried to drift down the stairs in Zora's fashion, but I bumped and thumped, frighteningly raw and broad beside her. "An honor, sir."

"Entirely mine," he said, and took my hand. "Lizzy spoke highly of you."

"She's too kind," I said.

"Do pardon me, ladies," Mr. Stewart said, with a step toward the door. Fairy lights played in his eyes as he told Zora, "I'm off to rescue your dinner party."

"Not Sebastian," Zora said plaintively.

"I have my intentions. Beware! Oh, my apologies, I meant—" He gave a little bow with a flourish. "Be well." And with a laugh, Mr. Stewart was off.

Cross, Zora hitched her skirts and stalked toward the stairs. "I know he's only teasing, but it's a given truth! Sebastian ruins everything."

Following her back up, I could do naught but inquire at the intrigue. "Does he?"

"Yes!" In the middle of her room, Zora spun and tossed

herself on the bed so completely that she'd need help back up. Though her corsets were looser laced for the day, she'd still be left to roll back and forth on the duvet like an upturned turtle. "First, he's a cousin, so he's no good for flirting with. Second, he's mad about an Araber's daughter and talks about her incessantly."

My trunk had arrived during our walk, and I opened it in search of something fresh to wear for dinner. "Is there a third?"

With a hand clapped over her eyes, Zora groaned. "Third, he fancies himself working class, which I suppose is closer to true than the lot of us imagining we're Astors, but he revels! He revels in rough suits and unkempt hair and dirty fingernails!"

"You sound entirely precious," I teased, shaking out my best overdress.

Sighing, Zora rolled, then rolled again, before giving up to sprawl on her back. "Mama says these are my dinner parties, but you see who arranges everything, don't you?"

"Let's then ask to manage the games afterward," I suggested, as if I had ever had a dinner party in my life.

Spreading her gown with her fingers, Zora sighed. "Mama would never."

"Beg it as a favor," I said. Then brightening, I unfolded my dinner skirt and turned to her. "Claim it's to educate me."

"You *are* dreadfully underschooled."

"Hardly fit for anything." Laying out my entire dinner dress, I stood back to consider it. "It would be a kindness, really. I'm nearly feral; what man would have me?"

"I read there's an orangutan on display in New York that wears a hat and smokes a pipe. Perhaps he would."

"For that, I should tip you onto the floor."

"Have I overstepped myself?" Zora asked.

And since I was a feral girl from the wilds of Maine, I offered my hand—and then tipped her onto the floor.

❀ ❀ ❀

The steady Mrs. Stewart from the docks had turned into a humming, buzzing whirl as we waited for the guests. Her skirts snapped as she moved from certifying the place settings to arranging Zora's curls against her cheeks. Then she turned to me with a distinct cloud of dismay.

"It's my best suit," I explained, trying to follow her with my eyes as she circled.

"And a well-done suit it is."

"She means it's unfashionable," Zora said.

"I mean it's a well-done suit." Mrs. Stewart reproved Zora with a sharp look. "Simply, the farther from London and Paris, the longer it takes to get the latest styles."

I stung with a fresh blush. I should have something gauzine and feminine like Zora had. She'd worn her tea gown all day, adding a shawl, a layer, a shell, until her morning breakfast dress had turned to formal dinner attire. It fit her softly, a vision in silk and lace.

Beside her, I was a great green beast. My suit only fit if my corsets were strung as tight as possible, so I stood breathless in heavy, peacock satin. From shoulder to thigh, my bodice armored me—a quilted shell in more of the same dour shade. I felt like our carriage at home, suitable for funerals and drudgery.

Finally, Mrs. Stewart clasped her hands together. She had no choice but to give up on me. "Pay it no mind, Amelia. You're our country guest; everyone knows that."

"What a terrible thing to say." Zora raised her hand to her lips, pretending shame.

"Did you offer her one of yours?" Mrs. Stewart replied, crisp again.

"She did, but they all came up too short."

Finally, Mrs. Stewart repeated, "It's a fine suit."

"You'll have new dresses soon," Zora added, slipping her arm into mine. "It's mostly family tonight, anyway. There's no one to impress."

Gray eyes rolling, Mrs. Stewart brushed past me to go check on the kitchen. She muttered under her breath as she went, which made Zora laugh.

"That wasn't awkward or uncomfortable at all," she said, petting me.

"It's almost like I belong here."

Eyes lighting again, Zora tugged my arm, and I turned with her. We spun slowly, a country mouse and a city mouse, and she waited until she'd ducked under my arm to say, "Don't you?"

❋ ❋ ❋

As Zora claimed, the dinner party was hers, even if her mother had decided everything from the menu to the china. Not a single guest could have been older than seventeen.

I'd never seen so many new faces at once, never shaken so many hands. Each one passed me to the next, their little novelty to entertain until they could return to familiar gossip on matters about which I knew nothing.

How would I ever remember so many names? I could scarcely breathe for the heat of so many people in such a small space. I found myself standing close to a window — shut, but the glass was cool where I dared to touch it at the sill.

All their voices mingled, spinning around in my head until the noise became a wall. I couldn't think because of it. I felt like I'd been dropped into a deafening silence, one that filled and emptied me at once.

As church bells tolled vespers, calling good Catholics to their evening prayers, I watched smoke rise in the goldening air. Sunset turned everything gilt. It made crimson edges of roofs and gables. All the pure white marble steps I'd admired on my walk with Zora now reflected amber.

Startled, I squinted through the light again. I swore, in all the gold, I saw dancers.

They rose like ghosts. At first, they skimmed through the air, stepping down the line in a reel. I curled a hand around my own throat, holding my breath now. I watched these unfathomable dancers sharpen, until I could make out faces! Familiar faces!

I saw Zora lower her eyes as she took a gloved hand. A spectral Thomas took wild liberties — his touch on her waist! Pulling her against his chest!

At once, phantasmal music filled my ears. Strings sang sweetly, high and crying, calling these young sweethearts to sway closer. Zora and Thomas turned through shimmering light, and I cried out when a real hand fell on my shoulder. It rent the vision like gauze, and I spun around.

"Our Fourteenth is here," Zora said, then added with concern, "I didn't mean to frighten you."

But she had. It was like I wasn't prepared to see her in the flesh, after so recently seeing her in a sunset reverie. She was no more golden than a bowl of apples, her gown nothing like the ornate confection I had just seen. Dreamed?

All the colors of the world had come back, but only because they had drained from me completely. Trying to gather my wits, I asked, "Is it Thomas?"

"No. He's *a* Fourteenth." Making the queerest face, Zora frowned, then recovered. "Papa hired him. I understand he paints."

We threaded through her guests to get a look at this hired guest, and I asked, "Houses?"

"Portraits. They all live in Mount Vernon Place. Bachelor painters and actors and such. Have them for dinner Friday, see them in the matinee on Saturday."

My smile grew curious. "All because it's bad luck to have thirteen?"

Zora shrugged. "We're civilized people."

"It makes me suspicious of your mother's culinary skills," I said, huddling on one side of the doorway to get a look. Already I could make out dark, waved hair and a suit that fit neatly. "That you should have to pay someone to round out the numbers."

With a pinch, Zora teased, "We're paying him to endure *you*, not the soup."

Thus far, I'd felt very clever in Zora's company, so I'm quite sure I would've said something witty if the Fourteenth hadn't turned from Mr. Stewart to look right at me.

Right into me.

Four

"Miss Stewart," he said, gliding past me to meet Zora.

I found myself plunged into darkness. Jealousy clasped me in its claw, an envy so raw and profound I wanted to weep with it. I decided I shouldn't ever let my imagination run away again, because it made me a terrible person. How could I burn with such covetousness, just because he introduced himself to my new friend?

"Nathaniel Witherspoon," he said, and bowed his head.

When he turned from Zora to me, the light went on again. His black eyes somehow cast me in the glow of a perpetual flame. He slipped his hand into mine, and I forgot how shocking and badly mannered that made him. I forgot everything but the mystery of his touch. He wore no gloves, and mine were only lace, so I felt his hand skin to skin.

"And you are Miss van den Broek," he said, and kissed my hand.

The warmth of his mouth bloomed across my hand, and his nails skimmed the inside of my wrist. Such great sensation for so little a touch; I had to struggle to answer him. "I am."

His face bore a hundred contradictions, round as the moon, but his jaw was handsomely sculpted. Thin lips held some claim on lushness, and his flat, almost messy nose flared with regal amusement when I failed to say anything more.

When he murmured, I felt his voice as vividly as I heard it. "Is the pleasure entirely mine?"

"Mr. Witherspoon," Zora reproved, and it distracted me how entirely ordinary she sounded. As if she had not noticed the buzz in the air.

Tipping his head, Nathaniel offered me his elbow. When I took it, the parlor lurched into motion again, into life again — suddenly, the sounds of conversation filled my ears. I felt the heat again of so much company, the floors rumbling with so many feet walking across it.

Clapping, Zora swept into the cloud of her friends and family, a dusky rose turning among them. "Shall we to dinner, then?"

Everyone else knew their order, and we filed into the dining room two by two. Nathaniel and I were left to wait for the last seats. Stolen glances told me so much more and yet nothing at all about the boy at my arm.

His suit was a deep shade of plum, one that masqueraded as black in all but the most direct light. His collar and cuffs were crisper than even Mr. Stewart's, held by enameled pins.

Only his boots betrayed him, pointing out that he was the starving artist Zora claimed all Fourteenths were. The leather shone, but it was cracked with age, and I wondered, by the way he walked, if they fit him at all.

Nathaniel brushed his head close to mine. "Will you be answering, Miss van den Broek?"

Catching my breath, I looked at him sharply. "I hardly thought you meant me to."

"I find rhetorical questions dull, don't you?"

Left gaping, I fixed my gaze on the candles burning on the table. Each flame danced, leaping merry high, making festive shadows across the china, and casting the most enticing lights through the crystal.

In my mind's eye, I could see again Zora's and Thomas'

golden dancing shades, and I shook my head to clear it. It seemed three days shipboard and an entire day of Baltimore's queer charms had unsettled me beyond all reckoning.

"If I may," Nathaniel said, slipping from me to pull out my chair.

Though I tried to say thank you, my words came out as a faint breath. He moved behind me, and I closed my eyes. I thought it would help steady me, but without the elegance of the table to distract me, I couldn't help but notice the spiced scent of his skin.

Rubbing at my stinging cheeks, I wondered if I could finish dinner but beg off the games afterward. I'd never been swallowed by emotion like this.

I admit, I'd never met many boys, and most of them just that day, but I was dizzy. I trembled, just because he stood near me. Surely Zora could see that I had taken a turn. Surely she would indulge me this once.

When Nathaniel sat, his gaze found mine again, and he said, *Are you troubled to find yourself so close to me?*

And forever I'd swear it—he spoke, and I heard.

But his lips moved not at all.

A March table was too early for flowers, so Mrs. Stewart had set out bowls of pinecones and fir sprigs, whole walnuts set off by black crescents—some sort of nut I'd never seen or tasted. Beeswax candles sloped from high to low in a joined arrangement, centered on a blue velvet runner.

With the eye tempted, nose and mouth followed—spices and salts, the dark, savory pleasure of roast duck set off by jellies in glass. Fish soups and lamb braises and damson tarts—it was so like the abundance of a Thanksgiving dinner that I struggled with the temptation to marvel. Instead, I sipped my tea and smiled at the conversation flying around me.

"Mama thinks we should roll the carpets back and host a dance ourselves," said Sarah Holbrook. She waved a hand to finish her thought. "Which is madness, plainly."

A gangling boy leaned over his plate. "It's always madness with you."

"He's right," another said. "This week it's hosting a dance, madness! Last week it was . . . what was it, Wills?"

"Why, Caleb, it was inviting Dr. Rea to morning tea."

"Madness!" they exclaimed at once.

Rolling her eyes, Sarah turned her plate with a smart twist. "I shan't say what else is madness, but it has to do with inviting donkeys to dinner parties."

Amused, I reached for my glass and found my knuckles skimming against Nathaniel's.

He ate with his sinister hand, and since the first soup service, his touch often collided with mine. When we held knives to cut meat, our elbows danced. My satin and his velvet whispered together. I can't say how distracting it was. I'd never been so aware of my own skin. I'd never known how quickly it could tighten with even a glancing caress.

"Apologies," he murmured.

"Accepted," I said, and I finished my glass.

Nathaniel moved to refill it with impeccable precision, manners *à la russe*. But as he held the decanter leftward instead of right, he slipped his arm beneath mine, tangling us intimately as he refreshed my tea.

How sweet a sting could feel! In my cheeks, in my lips — I found myself asking without a thought, with a light sort of amusement that came from some uncharted portion of my own wit, "What sort of schoolmaster did you have, who failed to beat you into using your proper hand, Mr. Witherspoon?"

His brow twitched, lips curled to keep a smile from coming on them too broadly. "If I said a blind one, would you blush?"

Heat flashed across my face, so it seemed the answer was yes. "Shame on you for wanting to embarrass me."

"Shame on you for indulging me."

Laughter rose with the clatter of china and silver, and I felt so very close to Zora's circle but not quite in it. It wasn't Zora's fault, because she addressed me often and encouraged her cousins to speak to me—once or twice with kicks beneath the table.

But she couldn't know that the light on her circle paled to the light in mine. Even when I looked at the cousins, admiring their smiles and pretty laughter, I felt myself drawn back to Nathaniel Witherspoon. And each time I caught him looking at me. At my mouth.

"Mr. Witherspoon, you're acquainted with the theatre," Zora said, cutting through our haze for his attention. "Have you heard anything about the Mysterious Lady Privalovna's engagement?"

And as if it were perfectly natural to be caught twined on a lady's arm at dinner, Nathaniel answered smoothly. "Only that you shouldn't miss it."

"Why is that, sir?"

"I'm given to understand that her spirits coalesce onstage. An ethereal mist drawn out of her for all to behold." To emphasize his point, Nathaniel fluidly swirled a hand in the air before him, unlatching us and performing all at once.

"Is that so?" Sarah asked, suddenly turned our way.

Zora reminded Sarah with a nudge, "Miss Avery promised that, too."

One of the boys groaned. "That was a waste of a nickel. Just at the climax, she claimed the spirits were too perturbed to materialize."

"Should've taken the warning at the window seriously. No refunds—for you'll be back asking for one, no doubt!"

Sarah frowned. "Just once I'd like to see a real one! It's tedious, wasting money on false spiritualists."

One of the boys cackled. "It's not madness?"

The table exploded in laughter, and they disappeared into familiar jests and stories only they knew. I was outside their consideration and wonderfully alone with Nathaniel again. Offering a smile, he raised his glass and his gaze to me once more.

And I drank deeply.

After dinner, we girls retired to the parlor while the boys converged on the back porch. They shouldn't have been smoking, though the sweet scent of tobacco crept into the house, nonetheless.

We shouldn't have stolen tastes of the sherry, but there we were at the fireside with one glass to share among us. There was wine at dinner, and that should have been more than enough spirits for any party. But all the same, with surreptitious dips of the crystal decanter, Zora handed around seven tastes in quick order.

"I'm not entirely well," I said when the glass finally came to me.

But I caught a glimpse of myself in the marbled glass above the mantel — tall, rough, rustic — surrounded by glorious Baltimore belles who each seemed like her own jewel set on velvet.

Sarah Holbrook shone as if she were summer itself. Her skin was bronzed chestnut, her hair rich black, braided into loops and weft with white ribbon. Beside her stood Matilda Corey — Mattie — another cousin perhaps, I had lost track in the introductions. She was Sarah's ghost in every way — platinum-haired and milk-skinned, her ribbons scarlet.

Their gowns bared their shoulders. Seed pearls and chokers made their necks seem that much more slender. I was the plain center of the blossom, buttoned to the chin in an old-fashioned suit and gloves of no remarkable style.

Kindly, Zora moved to pour the sherry back into its bottle, but I changed my mind. I took it and swallowed my portion in two sips. Smiling with a braveness I didn't quite feel, I said, "Now I'm fortified, I think."

"Good! Let's call the boys in," Sarah said.

She led the march—she on her toes and the rest of us following in kind. At the back door, we pressed in to listen, trying to steal snatches of the masculine conversation taking place just outside. I couldn't make much of it, only that they were loud and wild, and most certainly burning away cigars like they were grown men.

Rocking on her heels, Zora stole a look at Sarah, a portent of some ritual trick to come. Anticipation and a dash of sherry warmed my face, and I watched Sarah turn the doorknob slowly, squinting when the latch gave with a click. In quivering silence, we all stood, then Sarah began to count beneath her breath.

"One, two," she said, barely containing laughter, "three!"

She threw the door open, and our party—the ones familiar with the trick—screamed in a single banshee wail.

Orange embers scattered, dancing like fireflies. I saw the boys loping through the yard, dousing their cigars and catching their breath from the start. We dissolved into laughter as those nimble, timid boys came sheepishly back to the porch.

"Good luck marrying you lot off," Caleb said, narrowing his eyes at Sarah in a way both familiar and intimate. He passed close to her, a breath away.

Watching those two, I felt like I'd pulled the curtains back on their bed, as if I'd intruded on a moment meant only for them. When they slipped inside, I shook my head. Travel and wine and fantasies had addled me, plainly.

Nathaniel came in last.

Silently, he offered his elbow. It was maddening, how unsteady that simple gesture left me. It was like I needed to take it to keep myself on my feet. Slipping my arm through his, I looked at the floor instead of his face. I didn't want him to realize I was blushing again.

"May I call on you?" he asked.

Courting had rules. I didn't want to follow them. But I did, because I hadn't even spent an entire day in Maryland. When Lizzy and August sent me to find a husband, they certainly meant for me to find someone suitable. Someone with prospects. That discounted an artist making ends meet on hired dinners.

Ruination before midnight, before a single gown bought, before one seat won at classes? No matter how strange the day, I couldn't disgrace myself for the charm of one wicked Fourteenth.

Finally, I shook my head. "You may not, Mr. Witherspoon."

"Would you call on me, then?"

"You're mad."

"I'm fascinated," he said.

And, oh, it was no idle fascination. When he spoke, he looked not at my eyes, but at the curve of my brow. His gaze washed over my face. I saw him make out the shape of my lashes, turning his head to study my cheeks. He lingered long at the part of my lips.

Exposed by his consideration, I slipped from his arm and told him unconvincingly, "Miss Stewart will be missing you."

"I wish Miss van den Broek would miss me instead." He touched his palm to his chest and gave a little bow before walking around me. But instead of turning toward the parlor, he made his way to the foyer.

Laughter and accusations rang out from the parlor, some diversion already at its start, but I ignored Zora's guests to follow him. With only one lamp glowing, the air was a hazy, glowing curtain, and I caught my breath when I saw Nathaniel slipping into his coat.

Pointing the way, I said, "The games are beginning."

Nathaniel raised an envelope, holding it between us. "My wage is for making up numbers at the table. I'm not invited to the games."

He couldn't leave, not yet. I couldn't stand the idea of playing snapdragon with Zora's cousins, all those strangers, all alone. Then I had to wonder at myself—how had Nathaniel Witherspoon captured me so completely? I wasn't even startled to hear myself demand, "What if I wish it?"

He shook his head at me slowly, like a lament. Tucking his wage in his pocket, he met my gaze and said, "It was a pleasure, I hope."

A flutter rose in my chest. "You're going."

"All good things . . ."

There was a moment to say something, but nothing came. Did the slant of his eyes mean anything at all? All these games were new to me—how could I know the difference between a charming façade and an earnest heart? I couldn't begin to.

Swallowed by the most curious numb, I watched him go. It was like I had known the fierceness of the sun once but could remember it only faintly.

Knotted inside and out, I opened the door to call after

him, bid him call on me, or leave his card, or anything at all. But there was no one to hear me.

The street was empty.

※ ※ ※

Bundled beneath the sheets, Zora and I bumped and squirmed for possession of the middle. I suppose we were both spoiled, since neither of us had ever had to share a bed. But lying awake had its advantages—namely, the pleasure of gossiping in the dark.

"I think Wills is fond of you," Zora said. She bounced as she rolled over, making the mattress groan on its ropes.

I peered over my shoulder. "Which one is Wills?"

"The exceedingly tall one. It's good he fancies you this year. Last year he was a scarecrow in a suit." Suddenly, Zora leaned over my shoulder. Her face glowed in the moonlight, turning her into an otherworldly vision that would have frightened me if she hadn't crinkled her nose in delight. "We're waltzing this week-end. Dare you to put him on your card."

"I can't."

"I'll teach you," Zora said, exasperated.

This once, though, it wasn't my country manners keeping me from city pleasures. "I know how to dance, thank you!"

"Then what's the matter?"

Nothing. I just didn't want to dance close to someone I couldn't remember without help. I shook my head, as much an answer as I could offer, then said, "The funniest thing happened when we were waiting for dinner."

Zora grew wary. "Charlie didn't bother you, did he?"

"Which one's Charlie?" I asked.

In truth, I had some vague idea which cousin she meant, so I deserved it when she shoved me. But I had to clap a hand over my mouth to keep my giggles in. Outside our room, footsteps crossed the stairs. We must have roused Mrs. Stewart with our laughter. We held our tongues until the night watch had passed.

Once it had, I murmured, "I was looking out the window, right when the vespers bells tolled. My thoughts drifted, and I saw you. In a new dress."

This was hardly the relevant bit of the vision, but it suddenly occurred to me that perhaps I should test Zora's patience for supernatural whimsies before admitting mine. I wasn't sure about it.

It was a singular event. I'd never been struck by premonition in Maine, never had the slightest sensation of it. Spiritualists and séances and reincarnations were fashionable. Considering my anxiety, I might have simply retreated into a hundred stories I'd read before in magazines.

So this vision, of Zora in lilies—I decided to let her think I wasn't too serious about it. What if it turned out to be nothing but gilt-edged fantasy? How stupid I would feel.

"Was it a very good dress?" she asked. "I picked one from the *Harper's* book, but Mama said it would have to wait. It called for twelve yards of Irish lace. Twelve! But it was glorious!"

With a light smile, I said, "I hope it has lilies embroidered on the sleeves. That's the dress I saw you in, dancing with Thomas."

"It does! The entire polonaise is lace, embroidered with lilies!"

"Twelve yards!"

The bed groaned again when Zora pulled me to sit with her. She clutched my fingers, imploring with wide eyes. "Did you see it, really? All of it?"

I abandoned my studied lightness at once. "All of it," I swore.

With such earnest desperation, Zora stirred a heat inside me, an ardent hope that my sending would come true. Such a sweet soul, such a pure longing.

She deserves it, I thought. *Wanting something that badly should make it true.*

Then, as if she couldn't bear the possibility, Zora sighed and fell back on her pillow. "Thomas never comes to dances. Just another one of his mysteries, I suppose."

"This time, he shall." I pulled my pillow in my lap. "Once you have your dress."

"The twelfth of never, then." Zora murmured something to herself, then tugged my sleeve. "Lie down, dreamer."

As I lay back, I asked thoughtfully, "What do Four-teenths do, besides round out the numbers and pursue their arts?"

"Were you taken by him? Truly?"

"It was only a question." Punching the pillow, I stuffed it beneath my head and turned my back to her.

Her mood changed; I felt her soften. She tugged my braid and said, "They do what they like, I suppose."

I tried to imagine that—Nathaniel doing what he liked. It shouldn't have been hard. I wasn't caged myself. Lessons, yes, learning to turn out a hem and braise oxtail, indeed, but at Oakhaven I was given to my whims.

Any book in the library was mine to read. I had a pretty little charcoal set and new paper to draw on. There weren't any diversions to be had back home—no one my age to talk with—but I had no bonds, either. There in Baltimore, it seemed I could go calling, go prome-nading, even go dancing. Was that not doing entirely what I liked?

"I can't picture it," I said. I rubbed my throat, as if coax-ing words from it. "Can I confide in you?"

"Of course."

A painful stitch caught in my heart, and I said, "It's like he formed from the mists on our doorstep and dissipated into them when he left. As if he only existed when he looked at me."

When Zora didn't answer right away, I worried. What a mad thing to say out loud, about a stranger, at that. But then, with another tug on my braid, Zora said, "You know he's really got no entrance to our circle, don't you?"

"Yes."

"But you wish he did, nonetheless."

Pressing my hands against the absurd ache in my chest, I nodded. "Yes."

Zora leaned her head on my shoulder, then laughed and bounced back to her side of the bed. The pretty lilac scent of her powder drifted across me as the sheets settled in her wake.

"Cheer up, then," she said, a smile in her voice. "We'll find a way."

Five

I WAS EMBARRASSED TO FIND myself sitting in the last seat at Swann Day School. From my post, I admired the back of every head in class, including the glossy curls of a little girl who had two front teeth missing—she couldn't have been more than seven.

"Jumps," Miss Burnside told me as I watched Zora sweep to the front of the class, "may be earned on drills, each Monday morning."

As it was Thursday, I had no choice but to keep my wool manteau for warmth and haunt my sad desk in the dark. A round little boy recited his Latin—*amo, amas, amat*—

elementary conjugations that nonetheless he stuttered when he tried to slip from present tense to past.

Since I read from Cicero fairly well, I didn't need that lesson. I tried to concentrate on one of the others and nearly dozed. I had little inclination to calculate and no one to write to, so I looked around for entertainment.

Zora sat in the head seat, working figures on her slate. Though she moved through them ably, I noted that the empty seat beside her drew her attention again and again. Her skin seemed pale against the sapphire collar of her gown, as if she'd bathed in milk and moonlight. Her pallor troubled me somewhat, just because it was so stark.

Yet, I reminded myself sternly, she was nothing but the picture of health when we were playful or misbehaving. Class work would hardly bring the same roses to our cheeks as a game of forfeits, would it?

When the door behind me swung open, a brittle wind reminded me that I sat very far from the wood stove, indeed. It would have been rude to twist about in my seat, but I was entitled, I thought, to look up when the intruder passed. Cold came off of Thomas Rea's serge coat; I smelled it on him—a crisp touch of winter.

He stopped very near me and bowed to Miss Burnside, his hat in hand. "Forgive me, ma'am. Dr. Rea needed me in his surgery."

What a melody his voice made, throaty like a mourning dove, full of weight and shadows. On hearing him speak, at last I understood why Zora pressed herself against his fences, his name an oath on her lips.

Touching the reciter's shoulder, Miss Burnside peered at Thomas with the coolest of considerations. "You have come just in time to depart again with your lunch pail."

"I left it at home," he said. "I'll work through, to account for missed lessons."

Miss Burnside clasped her hands together. Not altogether young, but not so terribly old either, she wore a cloak of weary irritation as she returned to her desk. "Am I to sacrifice *my* dinner because you couldn't join us at nine o'clock?"

Zora twisted toward Miss Burnside, and I could tell from the flickering at her temple that she had an admirable defense she longed to mount.

Beside me, Thomas curled like an autumn leaf and said, "Never, ma'am, I apologize. I'll come back on time on Monday."

Lifting my hand, I spoke out of turn. "Miss Burnside, may I challenge his seat?"

"I'm quite sure I was clear, Miss van den Broek. Jumps are made on Monday mornings."

"Beg pardon, ma'am, I know." I felt quite in the middle of it—like I had a thousand eyes on me, for how bare I felt. I rose to my feet because I couldn't bear ignoring that bit of etiquette, too. "But it's empty now and wouldn't it be punishment enough if he had to take mine?"

The room stirred. Edwina Polk, one of the other girls our age in class, cast incredulous looks at Zora, who spread her fingers to cover her lips. Wills watched and Charlie smiled—only the littlest ones held their tongues. Their toes, instead, whisked the floor in a nervous rush.

With all grace one would expect of a lady, Miss Burnside said, "Perhaps you should like to teach my class?"

"No, I shouldn't like it at all, ma'am," I said, and flushed when laughter erupted. I hadn't meant to be impertinent. But I heard my smart tone, one I had always reserved for tormenting August. I bungled it all the more when I quickly added, "I only intended to have his seat."

Details turned sharp. Thomas' breath rattled as it drained out, and I heard Zora whisper, "Oh, Amelia." My manteau suddenly bestowed such heat that I longed to tear it off. Instead, I stood straight to await a reprimand.

Miss Burnside unstoppered her inkwell. She sat, reached for a pen, then pondered a moment. When she finally touched the nib to paper, its brass scratch seemed to claw my skin. I could scarcely imagine what terrible thing she needed to write at that very moment. I watched with a dawning terror as she tossed sand on the page to blot it, then blew it dry. Then she turned not to me, but to Zora.

"Miss Stewart, this is for your father," she said, folding her note in half. "You and Miss van den Broek are dismissed for the day. You too, Mr. Rea. Please show yourselves out."

❀ ❀ ❀

"Beg you forgive me," I said, clinging to Zora's elbow as we stepped into the cold.

The row houses had a curious effect on the wind — when it twisted between the brick narrows, it *cried*. How eerie a day so bright could be; how thoroughly I had ruined it trying only to help.

"Papa will . . ." Zora said, then trailed off. She looked

down one way, then the other, taking off suddenly as she finished her thought. "Well, he'll find it amusing. Mama, however . . . oh. I can hear her now."

I recognized our direction. She had turned us not toward Kestrels but toward the path we took last time, to spy on Thomas. Tugged along like a toy on a string, I followed Zora to the alley.

"I'll take the blame for it; it was my fault, not yours."

Dismissive, Zora said, "It gives us something to talk about. Thomas!"

Thomas stopped, making a tall shadow against the light at the end of the way. Perhaps I had infected Zora with my lapse of sanity, because I couldn't believe her. Where was the girl who'd introduced me to Thomas Rea behind the privacy of a fence? Why, she ran after him now—she called out to him!

When Thomas realized who called to him, he hesitated. I saw it in his step and the way he tipped his head to one side. Then finally, slowly, he approached us. It was a brave and dastardly thing to do, meeting a lady in an alley.

So that, perhaps, explains why he held a hand up to stop us a few paces from him. "Is something the matter?"

Zora slipped away from me. "I'm furious! Had you dawdled this morning, surely you'd deserve a reprimand, but working in the doctor's surgery!"

"No need to get inflamed about it," Thomas said. Then, his strange face turned with a smile. "Not so loud, either."

Softened by his remonstration, Zora clasped her hands together and said, more conversationally, "Miss Burnside's gone all twisted with power, and don't think I won't mention this to Papa."

"Please don't," Thomas said. He drifted nearer her.

"Why not?"

Closer still, as if a line between them tightened, Thomas said, "It was only an excuse, Miss Stewart. I held the man down and Dr. Rea had his tooth out well before eight this morning."

The clouds above us shifted, and lances of cool, clean light pierced the alley. Sounding betrayed, Zora asked, "Then why were you late?"

"I didn't care to sit her class this morning." Wickedly pleased with himself, Thomas started to say something else, but he took notice of me and turned formal. "We haven't met."

"This is my cousin, Miss Amelia van den Broek," Zora said. "She's come to stay the season. Amelia, Mr. Thomas Rea."

Remembering my wild flare of jealousy the night before, I kept my hands in my muff, offering a nod instead. "Good to meet you, Mr. Rea."

"Likewise." His eyes were green as glass. He looked from my face to Zora's, then said, "Now I understand."

Zora lingered beneath his gaze, her hands poised to raise her hood again but stilled in the moment. They seemed very like an etching, a modern-day Tristan and Isolde, whispering with their eyes.

But I ruined the atmosphere with my very presence.

Brought back to life, Zora arranged her coat and said, ordinary as anything, "We're taking a horse car to Old Drury, Thomas. Will you escort us?"

"He can't," I gasped. "Miss Burnside sent us home."

Zora sniffed and said, "On the contrary. She dismissed us and gave me a note to carry. She demanded no receipt."

"I shouldn't," Thomas said.

With a great rustling of satin and wool, Zora gathered herself, performing that most remarkable trick of making her pixie delicacy fill the space all around us. "Amelia and I chaperone one another. It's just that Holliday Street is so close to the Inner Harbor. I'd hate to fall to prey for want of a gentleman's protection. But certainly I understand if you don't care to offer it."

With that, she took my elbow and made me walk with her, a formal march betrayed only by the nervous flutter of her lashes. Halfway down the alley, she whispered to me, "Is he following us? I can't hear over my head's rush."

I tossed a look over my shoulder and smiled.

Of course he followed. After a performance like that one, how could he resist the encore?

❀ ❀ ❀

"They should tear this place down," Zora said, leaning into my seat to avoid a steady drip from the roof.

Though the marquee proclaimed this ramshackle mess the Holliday Street Theatre, it had earned the appellation *Old* Drury quite honestly. A moth-bitten rug lined the way from doors to stage, but several floorboards were missing.

That made the walk to our seats far more exciting than it had to be. And poor Thomas, he'd done his utmost to keep a respectable distance, only to find himself handing us down the aisle.

Grateful for the padding my skirts made, I still winced when my cracked seat threatened with a groan. "Honestly, do they light those sun burners?"

"They do." Thomas draped his coat over Zora's chair, to soak up the offending pool of water. His seat was none better—he sat at the edge, his knees pressed against the row in front of him. "And the pots onstage. There's an arc light up top, too. It gets black as the devil on Sunday nights, from all the smoke."

It was very nearly that black now, but mainly because the theatre had no windows. Recessed alcoves on the walls boasted gas taps furnaced in glass. Their glow lent just enough light to make out the crowd. A ribbon of incense tickled my nose, sweet over the rank cologne of mildewed theatre and damp wool.

"I hope Lady Privalovna manifests," Zora said. "Miss Avery was a disappointment."

"Aren't they all?" Thomas replied.

I think Zora would have said something more, but the ushers appeared. Their hard steps echoed through the theatre, and they shushed us as they turned the gas lamps low. Once they did, we would have been lucky to find our own hands in the resulting dark.

How exhilarating to be away from home, guarding our own virtue, in a pitch-black that surrounded us with strangers—with men! I felt a new fever in my blood; my skin hummed with it, and I murmured aloud in pleasure when a crack of lightning illuminated us.

From a hanging curl of smoke, Lady Privalovna appeared.

Then a blinding light from above spilled on her, and, oh, what a strange beauty she was! How shameless! Her loose hair cascaded over her shoulders like flaxen waters, bare and unpinned for all to see. And then, oh! Her figure was quite accentuated by the robes she wore.

She shunned her corset, letting silk follow her body, rather than forcing her body to follow the silk. Thus, when she came to the front of the stage, all her flesh wavered, shockingly unrestrained.

Gold and silver hoops weighted her bare arms. I thought at first they were made of some incredible singing metal, but then I caught a glimpse of her bare feet. She wore bells!

"Zora," I murmured, slipping my hand into hers. Lady Privalovna was the most provocative creature I'd ever seen. I felt quite glad I couldn't see Thomas' face, for I feared I would have been shocked to see a boy's reaction to such excess.

She answered my touch with a reassuring squeeze.

"I hear you," Lady Privalovna squeaked, brushing at the wild thicket of her hair. Her eyes opened until the whites shone all around the irises, and she rushed to one side of the stage. "I hear you, friends, spirits, guides! I await!"

Any murmurs left in the crowd melted away. Though I wondered that someone named Lady Privalovna should have no accent at all, I was enthralled. Incense grew thicker as she ran to the center of the stage again. She threw her arms out. Her head fell back, and she made a guttural noise that raised the hair on the back of my neck.

"Take this vessel!"

Rocking and rocking, Lady Privalovna became a pendulum. The silken tassels that pinned her gown to her shoulders washed back and forth, mesmerizing points between the flash of her bracelets. Her bells sang; her chest heaved with deep breaths. I couldn't look away. I couldn't imagine that anything else existed but this pale and terrifying medium.

She staggered, and a thick, white presence poured from her mouth. A lady close to the stage screamed. Men rushed to help the fainter as the manifestation swirled like milk in tea, up toward the ceiling to disappear.

The bells jangled, and Lady Privalovna staggered. She heaved, as if some hook had caught her and jerked her toward the heavens. Yellow butterflies poured from her. They danced around her head, flickering, fluttering, as the crowd swelled. It was like our voices had to follow them, as they melted into the dark.

Suddenly, Lady Privalovna stopped. She turned wild eyes on us and demanded, "Who is Jane? Which of you is Jane, oh gods, how the spirits cry." Clutching her temples, she rolled her head. "Show yourself, Jane, whose father is lost, show yourself!"

The dark made it impossible to see this Jane, but we heard her. Her seat snapped closed when she jumped from it, and her quavering voice carried over our heads. "My father is lost! This past winter at sea."

"The tides!" Lady Privalovna collapsed at the edge of the stage. She stayed us with a trembling hand, held high above her head. "No, no, let the spirits come through me, stay back! I bid you, disturb them not!"

Quavering with her, I held my breath and stared. What a terrible silence it was, waiting for her to stop panting, waiting for her to raise her golden head again. My hand grew hot in Zora's, and I took it back to clasp with my other, cold from clutching the damp arm of my seat.

I heard tears in Jane's voice when she dared to ask, "Can you . . . Do you see my father, good lady?"

"I do not," Lady Privalovna croaked, struggling slowly to her feet. "My guides, my friends, they speak of the tides! Of a shipwreck. Of a distant shore. Jane! Oh, Jane, they beg you listen!"

"Yes," Jane cried, sobbing.

Lady Privalovna peered out at her and said, "Your father is—"

Her eyes rolled back in her head, bracelets and bells all but screaming as she started to shake. She twitched and howled, a seizure sweeping through her like fire. That unearthly sound stole my breath; it pierced my heart and left me shaking.

And then she collapsed.

It was no gentle fall. Her head cracked against the stage—again and again. So did the heels of her feet, her whole body drumming the bare wood. Her arms twitched like snakes, and she thrashed ceaselessly across the floor.

Two men ran out. One slid to his knees beside her, leaning over to press his hand between her teeth. The other turned out to us and called, "Do not be alarmed! Please, do not be alarmed! This man is a doctor!"

With the stage in tumult, the crowd whispered a panicked hiss. We pressed forward; we watched in greedy anticipation to see what would become of the medium, whose fit had only begun to subside. The men spoke, too low to be heard. Then the doctor slipped his arms beneath Lady Privalovna's body, hefting her up.

"She has seen all she can bear today," he told us.

His companion held up hands to still the anxious murmur in the audience. "We beg your understanding. It's for the lady's health! We must insist she depart."

Just when feet started to rustle on the floor, Lady Privalovna rose up in her doctor's arm. She vomited a blue cloud that enveloped them. Her thin voice cut through the crowd with one last shriek. "The tides!"

The light died.

The performance was over.

Six

I'VE NEVER SEEN such a thing in all my life!"

Oh, the color had come back to Zora's cheeks! It had spread to the tips of her ears, too, which perhaps guarded them against salt-tasting winds that came off the nearby harbor.

We crowded outside the theatre, watching for a cab to carry us back to Reservoir Hill. Like a little bird, Zora stepped off the curb, then back on it, her eyes dancing again as she looked to me, then to Thomas. "Have you ever?"

I shook my head, stuffing my hands deeper into my muff. My head felt full, as if it might split with everything new poured into it. "Never."

"I've seen a fit before," Thomas said. He had a measured weight in his words. "But nothing like that, I'll give you."

"And that poor Jane!" Zora spun around again to study the crowd. "I wonder which one she is?"

A cool prickle rushed along my spine, like a winter wind dipped down my collar to torment my skin. Before I could consider it too much, a familiar voice answered Zora, and my skin stung after the chill.

"None of them, likely," Nathaniel said.

Newly pinned to the ground, I stilled. I believed, very much in that moment, that he had somehow slipped from the bonds of his skin to find me ethereally. My delusion of such an intimate connection was broken when Thomas looked past me, behind me, and said, "These ladies are in my charge, sir."

"A noble task you bear admirably," Nathaniel said, coming round to stand in the street before us. He offered Thomas a thoughtful look and then his hand. "Dr. Rea's boy, are you not?"

Restless, I ate up his details. This was my first glimpse of Nathaniel doing as he liked. And it seemed what he liked was lighting up a street by audaciousness alone. Gone was his staid, plum suit. Nathaniel stood there, bright as a poppy in winter. His coat was cut in green and gold tartan, and he'd pinned the pocket with a nosegay of tangerine silk.

Thomas read a nod of approval from Zora, then took Nathaniel's hand. Still, Thomas kept his guard, his jaw tight when he replied. "I am. Are we acquainted?"

"Once, I came to sketch an autopsy in your parlor."

I shivered at that awful remembrance. Even though it was common for artists to draw bodies in repose, it unnerved me to hear Nathaniel say it so casually. But I suppose it was just me, because recognition lit Thomas from within. "Mr. Witherspoon, of course."

Formality dispensed, Nathaniel said, "How did you find the show?"

All but exhaling her entire breath, Zora clutched my arm and said, "It was terrifying."

"And brilliant," I said. "The manifestations!"

"All a fraud, you know."

Unsettled as much now as I had been at dinner, I shook my head. "Were you there? Did you see?"

With a quick glance, Nathaniel leaped onto the walk and gestured for us to follow. "Come along, won't you?"

"We shouldn't," Thomas said.

"On my honor," Nathaniel replied, "nothing will come of this but revelation."

I think I would have followed Nathaniel anywhere, to

see nearly anything. The promise I had made to myself, to keep my wits about me, dissipated the moment I felt his voice on my skin. Thomas resisted at first. He didn't move when Zora and I started to walk. Zora cast him an imploring look, and then he followed, too.

Leading us through another alley, Nathaniel helped us over puddles of unmentionable provenance. I couldn't imagine what gave this passage a scent so pungent; it stung my nose and troubled my eyes.

"Act as though you belong," Nathaniel advised, and we found ourselves at the back of the theatre. Someone had propped a door open with a little iron dog. I smiled at that bit of whimsy and watched stagehands come in and out. They carried painted parapets and a shaky balcony, all light enough to lay on their shoulders.

Zora murmured to me as we watched an Egyptian column disappear into the theater, "There's an engagement of *Antony and Cleopatra* next week."

Though I found the workings of a theatre interesting, its artifices sweetly humble in the broad of day, I couldn't fathom what revelation we were meant to take from this. A hundred papier-mâché gods could march before me, and I would only marvel at their clever construction.

"Patience, Miss van den Broek," Nathaniel said. His words stung like a silver kiss, a forbidden intimacy I would have refused had I known it was coming.

Risking myself, I looked at him and said nothing. But I braved the blackness of his eyes and the wildness of my heart. I stilled my face, making it smooth, and then thought — clearly — to prove or disprove his command of my mind. *Look away,* I told him. *Yield your gaze first.*

Did his expression change? Did his brow curve at the challenge, or did I simply wish it?

I had no answer, for at that moment Lady Privalovna burst from the stage door, followed by her doctor. "I'm black and blue all over, and you want another show?!"

"People complain, Peg." The doctor followed her, and I pressed my face against Zora's sleeve to keep from gasping aloud. In his left hand, a dancing, shimmering bit of blue fabric trailed — in his right, a silvery piece of the same.

They curled and danced like smoke in the air, impossibly light. I had never seen a cloth that delicate, but I had seen two apparitions during Lady Privalovna's performance — one white, one blue.

"Peg's complaining," Lady Privalovna exclaimed. She snatched one of the apparitions and twisted it. "They paid their money! They got what they come for!"

The doctor twisted his apparition, and soon both grace-ful, fluttering scraps disappeared completely. "And three shows a day, look. Two shows is good-enough money, but don't you want to get married?"

Laughing, Lady Privalovna—or, it seemed, Peg—took something from his hand and brushed past him. "I heard that about a hundred times now. It don't look like I'm ever gonna be done with this, so I say two shows a day and you get rich at my pace. Where are those butterflies?"

"Search me," the doctor said flatly, making no move to follow her back inside. Reaching into his pocket, he pulled out a pipe as his gaze trailed to us in the corner of the yard. "What of it?"

"Are these the auditions for the chorus?" Zora asked quickly.

The doctor shook his head. "They take auditions at the office, around that way."

Sweeping her skirts in a curtsy, Zora said, "Thank you," then turned to us. "Shall we, then, to the office?"

Nathaniel admired her with a smile, and my belly twisted once more with uncharitable jealousy.

❁ ❁ ❁

We walked to the far end of Holliday Street, where Nathaniel said we'd more readily find a hansom cab to take us home. Though the horse cars still ran, daylight had shifted, casting long shadows to the east and washing us with the sharp, revealing light of afternoon. Our adventure, not yet finished, had to end nevertheless.

"All right, I grant the manifestations were showmanship," Zora told Thomas' back, as he and Nathaniel went before us on the street. "But surely the fit . . ."

Thomas stole a look over his shoulder. "Hysteria, I imagine. Father treats it with patents and a clockwork *percuteur.*"

Dubious, Zora said, "That's an illness, then? You can't pretend an illness."

Nathaniel dissolved into a fit of coughs, and just before I could lay my hands on his back in a panic, he sprang up again, spreading out his arms to present himself, entirely well.

"Sufficiently motivated," I said, fighting back an open smile on the street at his theatrics, "I suppose one could pretend nearly anything."

"Not that," Zora insisted.

The same spirit that took me to challenge Miss Burnside rose again, and I said, "I wager I could."

"Ladies don't gamble," Thomas said, and was startled when Zora burst out laughing in response. To recover himself, he almost smiled and amended, "Well, they shouldn't."

Perhaps not, but I was beginning to appreciate a certain thrill found in misbehaving. Due all, I realized as that peculiar warmth spread through my veins again, to Nathaniel Witherspoon's timely appearance.

"Here's a cab," he said, jolting me from my shameless considerations.

And there was, indeed, a brand-new hansom pulled by a fine Arabian. The driver had taken special care—silver bells jingled on the horse's tack, and its mane was gaily braided with ribbons.

"Take this one, please," Thomas said, standing at the step and offering Zora his hand. "We'll find another."

Nathaniel squinted at him. "It's all the same direction."

"These are ladies," Thomas replied, and though he often seemed to shrink into himself, at that moment he rose up. "Have care of their reputations."

Settling into the seat, Zora gazed down at Thomas, fairy lights in her eyes again. She seemed like liquid ivory, her pretty face poured into the sweetest fondness for Thomas' gentility.

I probably should have been sweet on him and his fine manners. But, I admit, it thrilled me when Nathaniel gripped my hand too long, then reached inside the cab to settle my hems.

"Do forgive me," he said, eyes meeting mine as he brushed gloved fingers over my boot. "I've no reputation of my own, and I forget they matter."

※ ※ ※

"We should have a picnic Saturday," Zora said.

Brush in hand, she smoothed her hair, letting it tumble down her back in glossy waves. Undressed to her corset and framed in the window, she seemed so very like a water nymph from *Des Nibelungen* that I expected her to reclaim the ring at any moment.

Thimble in place, I bent over my mending. "I thought we danced on Saturday."

"Not in the afternoon." She switched her brush from one hand to the other, reaching for another thick length of hair. "It could be too chilly."

"If today was any indication, I agree entirely."

"How can you be so driven by the cold?" Zora asked

with a laugh. Slipping to her feet, she swayed toward me, taking soft, dancing steps to a melody she alone could hear. "Papa said Maine was ice from September to May, with a grudging admission of rain in the middle."

"I'll have you know, our summers are lovely," I said loftily. "For the entire afternoon that they last."

Twirling past, Zora reached for her house gown. "If it was archery, we could *coincidentally* practice near the pond."

Putting my sewing aside, I looked up at her. "Dare I guess the reason we should want to practice near the pond?"

"They fish, you know," Zora said, sweeping past me again, the dark cloud of her hair washing all around her and making her nearly exotic. "And sail toy boats, like they're children, and throw stones at their boats to sink them, like *foolish* children."

I smiled. "Thomas does, you mean?"

"All the boys. Overgrown and boisterous, the whole lot. The Fourteenths, too. I've seen them."

Oh, a hot, flashing grasp overwhelmed me, evident even in my voice. "An opportunity, then, to be seen."

"And incidentally socialize," Zora said. "They eavesdrop, and should we happen to mention there's a dance at nine o'clock, and where it might be . . ."

The grip round me loosened a bit, and I turned back to my thimble and thread. "And directions to the back doors and masks to disguise themselves."

"Show some spine," Zora said.

I laughed, for hadn't I? "Your mother didn't care much for the spine I showed our teacher."

"But Papa laughed and said it's no matter. Thus, it's no matter."

"Do you give your mother fits, I wonder?"

Zora tugged her robe closed and graced me with a smile. "I do hope it's so, for I'm very like her. She married for love, you know."

"I didn't."

"And now you do," she said, and gazed out the window.

When her lashes slipped low and her lips parted on a breath, I could see no reason why Thomas shouldn't propose at once. I wondered if I could ever be so polished, so ideal. I felt very far from that ideal, and I longed to approach it. But then a sudden, contrary fire lit inside me. What good did goodness do me? Nathaniel had no use for it . . .

"Do you think we'll come to our senses?" I asked suddenly.

Raising one finger to touch the glass, Zora traced a *Z* in the fog there and murmured, "I hope not."

Seven

I WAS BOTH ASHAMED and shameless to find myself offering Mrs. Stewart a lie. Though I trembled with an anxious rush, I looked right in my cousin's eye and said, "I'm only worried that if I wait until later, it will rain."

Mrs. Stewart glanced at the dark clouds, then turned to me. "I don't know about this."

"But it's just a block or two, isn't it?" I clutched the whole family's mail, holding it against my chest. "I've been remiss; I haven't mailed a single letter home yet."

"Will you be telling them you got sent home from school the first day?"

Heat stung my face, and I quailed. Truth was, I'd written

half a page about nothing in particular, except that I had arrived and the Stewarts were very fine people, indeed. Trying to guess at what answer she expected of me, I finally said, "I wouldn't want to worry them."

Cruel as cruel, she let me hang there a long moment in silence. Then she squinted at the weather again and relented. "Straight to the corner, a right, and then the next left. If you should get lost, ask a lady to direct you."

"Yes, ma'am," I said, half out the door.

"Take my umbrella. And don't speak to any men!"

Her warning echoed behind me, and my nerves were so excited, I almost tripped over my feet. Though the sky hung heavy over me, I felt impossibly light beneath it. *Look at me,* I wanted to cry—I wanted to spin in circles on the curb and laugh. *I'm doing what I like in the city!*

Plainly, I would have been drunk on my freedom, anyway. But the secret truth of my errand was still more intoxicating. Minding Mrs. Stewart's directions, I found the post office in short order and reveled in going into it alone.

How simple I must have looked, but I was entranced by the drawings of outlaws posted to the walls. As I waited in line, I lost myself to reading the descriptions of their wicked deeds. Murders, bank robberies—all terrible and, for their novelty, fascinating to me. Thunder rolled, atmosphere for my scandalized reading.

"I'd like to mail these," I said, when it was my turn to approach the window.

"See, you, get out!" the clerk shouted.

My face flamed. I turned to go, when he reached a crabbed hand out to catch my wrist.

"Not you," he said, leaning to peer around me. "That one!"

I turned just in time to see a little boy make a very rude gesture. He hardly reached my waist; I couldn't believe he was out of short pants, let alone loose in the city on his own watch. This was my first walk alone, and I was barely sixteen!

The boy hopped onto a bench, puffed with tiny bravado. "It's raining out there, innit?!"

"Then go lay about the telegram office!" The clerk hesitated and then slammed a CLOSED sign on his window. He disappeared, only to burst from a door with a broom. "This here's the federal government, you gibbous brat. No loafing! Out!"

I clapped a hand over my mouth to silence a gasp. But the clerk didn't just threaten with the broom — he used it! He hit the boy with the brush end of it and swept him into the rain-dark streets. Then he returned to his side of the counter and smiled at me. "Where was we, hon? Posting some letters?"

With a nod, I pushed my bundle toward him. "There's one to Maine, the rest are Baltimore."

Mumbling to himself, he pulled out a measure and a tray of vulcanized stamps to get to his business. With him busy marking his ledger, I asked as innocently as I could, "Oh, sir, could you tell me how to get to Mount Vernon Place?"

I felt effervescent, a bubble that swelled as I waited for his reply. As I waited for directions that would take me to Nathaniel Witherspoon's door. I didn't intend to use them. Of course not, but I savored the wickedness in the asking.

"Halfway between here and the Inner Harbor," he grunted, pulling out a great mechanical stamp. He used all of his weight to work it, slamming the handle down to cancel the postage on each letter. "North Avenue car to Calvert Street. Visiting the Stewarts, are ya?"

Shivering, I wondered how he could know. Then, instantly sheepish, I realized—didn't he have my mail in his hands? "Yes, sir."

"Mr. Stewart's office is down about that ways."

The rain outside roared, and my heart pounded to match the thunder. My wicked bubble popped, and I swallowed nervously. What if the clerk mentioned my inquiry? How could I explain wanting directions that I didn't ask the Stewarts for? Oh, horror, I was so caught in the idea of the city that I forgot a neighborhood is no more than a small town in it.

Fishing my purse from my coat, I fumbled a few thick coins onto the counter. "Thank you kindly, sir."

"Enjoy your stay, hon," he answered.

The stamp crashed down again, filling my ears as I slipped, considerably dimmed, into the rain.

☀ ☀ ☀

Complaining bitterly, Mrs. Stewart herded Zora and me into the dressmaker's shop.

"After that performance at school, you're lucky I don't throw you in the cellar to grow eyes with the potatoes," she said, hooking her umbrella on the coat stand.

Since Zora kept her tongue, so did I. The trouble and the blame were all mine, and I couldn't argue that I deserved leniency for such bad behavior. And yet I got the most distinct impression that we were not so much contrite as making ourselves deliberately deaf.

The prismatic glory of a full wall of fabrics beckoned us near. I joined Zora in front of it, and we rubbed corners of velvet and serge, marveling at weight and hue. The variety staggered our senses. Sedate colors seemed to fade to shadows, because the upper selections screamed brightly with the new aniline dyes.

"Can't you just see a sheath of this," Zora said, touching apple-green satin, then reaching across to caress a cream brocade patterned with violet and pinks, "under a polonaise made of this?"

I nodded, but the sunny oranges and yellows drew my eye. They were so lush that I wished I could soak in all their warmth just by rubbing my cheek against them. Before I gave it serious consideration, the dressmaker came to greet us.

The script on the front window proclaimed that this shop belonged to Mademoiselle Thierry, but the woman who parted the narrow shop wasn't a miss at all. She wore her silver-shot hair in a tight crown of braids. Lines gracefully marked her walnut face with age. She nodded to Zora and me, but welcomed Mrs. Stewart with wide, gracious arms. The woman was no fool. She knew *we* were nothing but the mannequins to be dressed.

Her voice lilted, a marvel of an accent not quite French, but not quite Maryland, either. "What a day for necessaries, mm?"

"And one just started," Mrs. Stewart agreed, walking with her toward the back of the shop. "You got my note about our cousin Amelia?"

Mlle. Thierry nodded, pulling a huge book from beneath her counter. It landed on her cutting board with a thump, splitting open to the middle-most pages without bidding. "*Mais* yes, and I marked out these on your budget. It's the lace that troubles me."

"I have two yards besides on reserve," Mrs. Stewart said, which put that strange conversation to rest.

"Then all I need is my tape and"—Mlle. Thierry's voice rose, plainly intended to draw my attention—"this little *missié* to come to the back room. 'Zelle Stewart, you've kept that seal cape fine as the day it left my hands."

Warmed by the compliment, Zora nodded. "Always and always, mademoiselle. I treasure it. May I sit for the measurements?"

Mlle. Thierry waved us both back. "Hurry up. You heard your mother. A long day ahead, and I won't be the one to keep her. Hup, hup, faster, *s'il vous plaît.*"

So faster we went, and Mlle. Thierry left us alone in the back to do the business work while I undressed. Slowly, I hung my muff and cape on hooks. Dawdling, I folded my gloves, then finally stepped onto the measuring block.

"She's from New Orleans," Zora told me, working the endless string of buttons on my polonaise.

"I admit, I wondered."

Lowering to a whisper, Zora said, "I heard she held a salon there so exquisite that people clamored for invitations. Ambassadors and barons and every fine family in the city came. If she would see you, you were all but royalty!"

"How did she come to own a dress shop in Baltimore, then?" I asked.

"She doesn't speak of it." Zora stepped onto the block to help me and whispered in my ear, "But when she raises the measure over your head, look into her cuffs. Scars, awful ones."

I blinked at Zora. "Truly?"

"Oh, yes," she murmured, then shut her mouth before she was caught gossiping.

Something shadowed and uncertain prickled along my skin as we bared it, bit by bit. Trying to put thoughts of dark secrets and hidden scars from my mind, I sadly reminded myself that I was stripping off in public. Shivering, I clapped my hands together and gazed at the ceiling in a quiet sort of terror.

True, no one could see into the back room, but I felt unnatural. And cold—my skin tightened everywhere, a rush of chill on it. That made me feel all the more wanton and obvious! I tried to distract myself with my surroundings.

The stove in the corner threw off little heat, though the room was cheery in its own way. Pinned to the wall, fluttering scraps added color between big sheets of patterns marked in oil pencil.

I felt no small measure of envy that Mlle. Thierry had a sewing machine—a black, glorious monster worked by a foot pedal beneath it. Lizzy and I kept Oakhaven in clothes and linens by hand. My stitches were good—even and tight—but I guessed that an entire gown could come out of a machine like that in days, not the weeks it took me.

Appearing with a knotted rope, Mlle. Thierry circled the block, measuring first with her eyes. She hummed and *ah*-*h*ed, sounds meant for herself that nonetheless set my nerves alight. Did she find me lacking? Was I too tall to be fashionable? And on top of it, I felt like a gawker, constantly trying to peer into her sleeves.

She made a noise at me, which I took to mean I should raise my arms, and I did.

"Mm," she said, looping the rope around my waist, then quick as a sparrow, she raised it to span my bust. "Is your corset as tight as it goes?"

"Yes, ma'am," I said, cutting a plaintive look in Zora's direction. She answered with a shrug.

Mlle. Thierry hummed again, spanning my hips with the measure, before unfurling it to its full length and trailing it from my hip to my ankle. "Let's see your boots, 'Zelle van den Broek."

Puzzled, I rucked my skirts in my hands, lifting them and sticking my foot out for her consideration. In my estimation, my boots were quite fine—nearly new kid leather accented with black ribbon, turned out with black glass buttons.

But it seemed she cared less about the fineness of the construction than she did the height of the heel. "Not a full inch," she told herself, then stood. "Undress to the corset. *Je me reviens.*"

I said nothing; I only gaped at her, wide-eyed and open-mouthed, as she bustled into the next room again. Though I heard her speaking to Mrs. Stewart, I was too shocked to understand either of them. "To the corset?"

"Quit complaining," Zora said, on her feet again to help me. "I bet she's got a finished dress that might fit."

Fingers numb, I clumsily worked my ties and hooks. "Whose?"

"Yours, if we pay for it. If an order goes unclaimed, she'll sell it off at a discount. I got my cape that way." Zora gave me a pinch and squinted up at me. "Help me, you goose. This could be glorious."

Or it could be a disaster. With wary hands, I bared myself to find out which.

❄ ❄ ❄

On Saturday Zora and I abandoned our aprons for our capes and fled to Druid Hill.

"Cut across the lawn," Zora said, veering off the path and leaving me to follow or not. She wound through a cloud of toddlers in matching pinafores and bonnets. I scattered the darlings like little pink ducks, cutting down the middle and apologizing to their nurse as I passed.

Down a slope toward the lake, Sarah waved at us, as Mattie squinted beneath her gloved hand. Settled on a blanket, they seemed almost at picnic, except for the longbow. A target stood behind them, and Sarah looked wonderfully athletic in a suit cut just for archery.

"I wondered if you were coming," Sarah said, leaning in to press her cheek against Zora's and then mine.

Mattie squeezed my hand, with no more grip than the weight of a butterfly. "How do you do, Amelia?"

"Very well, thank you."

Zora picked up a nude shaft, one encumbered by neither arrowhead nor feathers. With a wink to me, she told Sarah, "This won't do."

"There are four in the quiver all ready," Sarah answered smartly.

"One for each of us?" Zora asked, giving me a nudge as she peered at the fletch works spread out before us.

"Is that how it's going to be? I bid you bring *your* quiver next time."

Sinking down at once, Sarah reached for the brush she'd left in a pot of glue. Mattie offered her a half-finished arrow. Hand steady, Sarah painted a slow, fine thickness of glue, then reached blindly for a feather to lay on it.

Zora took the longbow, hefting it until it curved neatly in her grip. "I'm showing Amelia how it's done. Have you seen anyone?"

"The two of you and no one else. It's been lonely."

Mattie sighed as she reached for another shaft. "I'm dreadfully slow when it comes to proper fletching."

"Oh, is this meant to be proper fletching?" Zora said, before asking Sarah, "Then why aren't you sewing those on?"

Sarah smirked. "If I wanted to sew, I would have stayed at home."

Much like her mother, Zora herded me with a tap—she, however, did it with the yew crook of Sarah's bow. The wood gleamed, an inviting crescent that was nearly as tall as we. Plucking two arrows from the quiver, Zora handed one to me and nocked the other against the bowstring.

"Like so," she said. She expected me to take in the details as she drew the string back. It hummed, the echo of a carillon when she released it, and the arrow gasped as it flew. It pierced the target in the biggest ring, hardly an ideal shot.

"Very good!" Mattie exclaimed anyway, clapping softly.

"Another," Zora said, holding out her hand for my arrow. "I have to get a feel for it."

Hiccupping with laughter, Sarah said, "Is that your newest excuse?"

Zora drew the string back again. "I'll have you know, I was made Flight Mistress that summer in Annapolis."

"You were eight, and they were coddling you." Sarah's nose crinkled when she smiled at me, lazily waving the newly feathered shaft before her face as if it were a fan. "Our Zora, she's a terrible sport."

"She just wants to do well," Mattie said, equivocating as she watched the latest shot fly.

"Another!" Zora said, and cursed when this one went wider still. When she realized I had nothing to hand her, she stalked over and emptied the quiver. She posed and drew back once more, cursing when this shot flew true and straight—and missed the target entirely.

"Fetch it," Sarah sang, laughing again when Zora pushed the bow into my hands. "This is but a taste of the glories of playing sports with Zora Stewart. Once she hit a lawn tennis ball so far off course, we never found it. Now we have to use a bed knob if we want a whole set."

"I fear for the replacement birdies in your badminton kit," I said.

Failing to grasp the sarcasm, Mattie said, "Oh, we use a bit of cotton stuffed in leather."

Since Zora hadn't yet returned, I decided to try the bow. It refused a gentle tug, insisting on brute force to stretch it. A twinge cut my shoulder, and I gasped in shock at the weight of the string. I was so determined that I spun with the exertion, turning as if the bow were my rudder.

Sarah ducked. "Keep it pointed away, please!"

"Beg your pardon," I said with a wince. Steering myself back, I aimed at the straw-stuffed target and promptly dropped the arrow. A boon, I thought, for Zora popped up like a clockwork monkey from behind it, waving her retrieved prize.

"Look what I found," she crowed, and when Nathaniel strolled up after her, I laughed.

Sarah gaped. "Did you flush him out like a woodcock?"

Nathaniel bowed to Sarah, his pursed lips twisting in a smile. "More like a turkey, I hazard. Miss Holbrook, a pleasure to see you again."

"And you," she said, a hitch there at the end, which Nathaniel kindly filled with his name.

His charm fit him as easily as his coat. Vulcan red with black velvet accents, silver buttons, and a white carnation pinned to the lapel—she should have called him a cardinal, and I intended to, if he ever noticed me. Mattie blushed a matching shade of scarlet when he took her hand.

Finally, at last, he bowed to me. "The always enchanting Miss van den Broek."

"Mr. Witherspoon." My voice came out unexpectedly soft.

Leaning against the tree, Nathaniel burned through me with a look. "I can fit the arrow points, Miss Holbrook, if you like. Don't let me disturb your party."

Zora brushed against my shoulder, murmuring as I raised the bow again. "He came out of nowhere, Amelia. I was entirely alone, and then . . . *ffft*, I was not."

He's very like that, I started to say, then remembered that I was pretending at competence. Struggling against the bow, I ordered it to stay true and still in my hand. Though I felt a tremor come through my arm when I pulled back the string, I ignored it and held my breath. But, perhaps, I forgot the most essential part of archery—my aim.

When Zora whooped, I opened my eyes. My little arrow had barely struck the target, a hand span from the rings.

"Very good, Amelia," Mattie said.

Handing the bow to Zora, I ran to retrieve my arrow. I stopped beneath the tree's empty bower, very near Nathaniel, it so happened. A coincidence, entirely.

"That was terrible," Nathaniel said, a honey murmur for my ears alone.

Playing at pride, I brushed my cheek with the arrow's feathers and replied, "How sad that you're driven to mock my incredible prowess."

"Head down," he said.

Zora's shot bounced off the board and went careening into the distance again. From her vantage, Sarah covered her eyes and said, "I think it's gone in the trees."

"Forgive my impertinence, ladies," Nathaniel said, looking around at us. "But have you considered a sport at which you might actually excel?"

"Hold your tongue, sir." Sarah held out her hand, waiting for him to take it and help her to her feet. When he did, she bowed, then plucked up the bow, sure as Artemis.

Confiding, Mattie turned to us. "She's got a knack for it, watch."

In the time it would have taken me to find the right end of the arrow, Sarah produced one from its leather case, drew it, and released it, a precise ballet set apart from our sorry attempts. The bowstring hummed, and Sarah's arrow whistled where ours had only whispered. It pierced the red inner ring of the target with a rush.

Nathaniel flashed his hand at me, three fingers tipped with silver points. The motion distracted me, the way it captured light or the graceful way his fingers curled. Or maybe it was just that they were *his* fingers. I forgot myself for a moment gazing at them.

He reached out, touching my chin with a cold point. "I believe she challenged you."

"I believe she educated *you*," I said, but pushed off the tree all the same.

"Take a breath," Sarah advised, passing the bow into my hands. "Keep your eyes open, then exhale as you release."

The very idea that I should be steady made me want to laugh. Nathaniel unsettled me when I held nothing more complicated than an oyster fork. Wasting time before I had to show myself inept again, I looked about and called, "Zora?"

"I can't find the blasted thing," she called back, straggling into sight in the distance.

Nathaniel said, "Is that a lady or a longshoreman?"

"In Baltimore, there's hardly any difference," Sarah answered.

Exasperated, I dropped the bow to my side and turned to them. "Both of you, for shame, I'm concentrating here."

Giggling softly, Mattie leaned her head on Sarah's shoulder to watch. Sarah, though, reached for her pot of glue once more, and said, "Should I do it for you, Amelia? I'd be happy to proxy if there's some point to be made."

"Thank you, no," I said, and posed once more.

Emulating Sarah, I pulled the string back with all my might. A surge rose in me like the scent of fresh earth but more primal. Like determination, only it spilled not from my thoughts but from my blood, my very bones. I breathed. I opened my eyes wide, and I fired.

A terrible scream rent the air. Inhuman and shrill, it crushed the breath right out of me. I threw the bow down and ran toward the target—begging, pleading, praying that somehow my arrow had not found its way into Zora's innocent flesh.

Sarah and Nathaniel rushed up behind me and caught me

when I staggered. My prayers had been horribly answered—the arrow hadn't found the target or Zora's flesh.

Instead, it pierced the breast of a struggling dove.

Its feathers blossomed scarlet all around the wound. It flapped helplessly, unable to fly. Suddenly, Mattie appeared at my elbow. She pulled my head against her shoulder, hiding me from the destruction I'd wrought.

"I'll take care of the poor beast," Nathaniel said.

I couldn't think; I couldn't breathe. I could only hear that tortured scream, ringing again and again in my ears, and I cried.

Eight

"IT'S STUPID, ISN'T IT?" I asked, bundled by the stove in my housedress, pearl-handled brush in hand. Zora sat at my feet, the full length of her hair spread in my lap. "I've done hens at home for dinner and cleaned fishes and hares."

"But when it's a hen, you meant to—that's the difference, I think."

Sunset glanced through our window, dipping Zora in a gold and crimson glow. When I closed my eyes, I saw her turned in a waltz again, lilies on her shoulders. I could all but hear the strains of violins this time. Before the waking world slipped from me, I shook off the vision.

Turning to my iron clasps, I considered them as they heated on the stove in a row. To change the subject somewhat, I asked, "Will there be another dance soon?"

"Twice a month, this sort, another two in Annapolis if we can convince Papa to drive," she said, scratching her nails against her knees in quiet anticipation.

I consulted the magazine splayed open on the table, then snatched a searing pin from the row. Waving it a few times, I pinched off a section of Zora's hair and rolled it quickly, before I blistered or she singed.

"I'm sorry to miss it, Zora. I wish I weren't so nervous."

Zora made no attempt to hide her discontent with me. She flicked a gaze back and said, "I'm sorry you're such a goose."

Consulting the sketch again, I squinted at the strange direction the next pin should take but followed it nonetheless. "I'm just so unsettled. How could I strike it? I didn't even see it!"

Tipping her head back in my lap, Zora peered at me. "It was a lucky shot, nothing more."

"How lucky I feel," I said, pushing her off my lap so I could brush out the next bit of her hair.

Mrs. Stewart backed into the kitchen. "Out of my way!"

"We're sitting at the stove, Mama," Zora called back

irritably. She chafed so at the oddest things, and I found them all endearing. To be so familiar with a mother that one could say any stray thought or vexation — I envied it. But I envied it sweetly; my heart was glad to be a part of it.

"Ungrateful you," Mrs. Stewart admonished, then stopped at the counter.

At first, it seemed she'd unfurled a literal white flag. But this one had the effect of sending Zora to her feet with a strangled cry. She rushed over, half-pinned, half-dressed, and raised the sleeves of an Irish lace polonaise.

Then at once, she dropped the sleeves. Crushing the new dress between them in her exuberance, Zora threw her arms around Mrs. Stewart. "Mama, you didn't!"

"More the fool I, I did." Mrs. Stewart didn't sound as though she felt a fool, though. Her face shone with delight over Zora's shoulder.

When she stepped back to shake the gown out, she tsked and ticked over it. It was a spectacle, luxurious silk and lace falling in a wonderment of fashion.

"Oh, thank you! Oh, you've gone mad! Can you put it in my room, please?" Zora asked, then turned back to me. "Amelia, now you *have* to go."

I shook my head. "Honestly, I don't think I feel up to it."

"Couldn't you change your mind?" Zora asked, sweeping back to me. She dropped to the floor, rather abruptly I thought. She slipped her arms beneath her hair, raising it all up at once to spill in my lap again. "Just to see it through?"

I felt the prickle of my portent as I reached for the brush. Call it pride, but if she waltzed with Thomas in her unexpected dress, I wanted to see it. How could I miss the chance to see my only premonition come true?

Winding her hair slowly around my hand to finish the pinning, I hesitated. "All right . . ."

"I win again," Zora cried, clapping her hands together.

"All right, but I don't intend to dance," I said. I tugged her hair, then reached for my next pin. I put the wounded dove from my mind, setting those thoughts to waltz steps instead.

Baltimore had a way of demolishing my good intentions, and I suspected I might end the night with a dance, after all.

Veiled by linden trees, the mansion on Garden Lane welcomed us with glowing gas lamps. This fine place belonged to a judge, and his friendship with Zora's father gave us entry.

"May I take your coats?" the doorman asked. Turning

gracefully, Zora slipped from her manteau, then surrendered her umbrella. I shied from him, taking in the rich wood walls, the pure perfection of arched ceilings.

The chandeliers cast glittered light on the guests, turning them magical. Ebony girls laughed with tawny boys. A russet couple stood beneath a grand bay window, stunning in their aniline silks and velvets. What a glorious place Baltimore was—the whole world in one city! In one parlor, and I had a ticket!

"Give him your wrap," Zora ordered me, snapping me from my amazement.

I turned to do just that but stopped short. "I can't go out there in this," I told Zora, pressing both of my hands to my shamefully bare chest. My wonder at the entire world turned to dread.

"You can," she answered smartly, "and you shall, this very minute."

Mrs. Stewart and Mlle. Thierry seemed convinced that this *damassé* silk fit me perfectly. In the shop I had agreed with them. I'd let the amber beading dazzle me. I'd slipped into the thrall of the brocaded satin train, the coppery plush pleats, oh, everything about it!

But standing in the foyer of a great party, under ample light and so many gazes, I couldn't bear it. With each breath,

I felt my bust rise, a great expanse of flesh for taking chills and salacious looks alike.

I had lost my mind, for in that moment, I wanted my green battle armor back. How I went from stuffy to wanton in the change of a single gown, I can't imagine. My reasoning verged on hysteria, but I couldn't rid myself of it.

"Amelia!"

"What will they think of me," I murmured. "What possessed me to wear this?"

Firmly, Zora took me in hand and dragged me to one side. It was awful; guests had arrived behind us. I'd unwittingly made a scene and made it worse by the moment.

"If it bothers you, keep your wrap." She spoke through her teeth now, baring a dangerous smile.

The blush that stung my cheeks burned to the bone. We both threw prettier smiles at an older woman who came through, one Zora sweetly greeted as Mrs. Bonds. As soon as she passed, I turned back. "I haven't got one."

"Take mine!"

Startled by her vehemence, I asked, "Am I driving you mad?"

"I just wish you'd enjoy this," Zora said. "It's a brilliant dress, worlds better than either of us could have afforded. Think of the attention you'll draw."

Muttering, I said, "I am. That's why I'm troubled."

"Amelia." Zora stood and shook me—truth be told, a bit harder than she needed to. "This is the only season girls like us get. I order you to savor this! It will all be gone soon enough."

"That sounds very like resignation."

"It's realism. What do the farmers say?" Zora asked.

Though I could tell she was quizzing herself, searching out the answer in her mind, I said, "I haven't the first notion. We Van den Broeks neither plow nor sow."

Rolling her eyes, Zora said, "Oh, dash you, then."

I threw my arms around her, enveloping her in a fond embrace. "Dash you right back."

She was right. We had to savor the moments granted us, for this one summer past childhood and before womanhood. If that meant scandalous gowns and tipping our lashes at boys, then so be it.

In the satin rustle of our hug, Zora suddenly exclaimed, "Make hay while the sun shines!"

With all made better, I could tease, "Your agricultural fascination troubles me, Zora."

❀ ❀ ❀

Between the upper and lower music rooms, I lost track of Zora. So many faces swirled around me, so many dancers took to the floor, that I felt quite compressed in all of them.

The noise and laughter and lights thrilled one moment, then terrified in the next. I took conversation where I found it and fanned myself in earnest when Judge Bonds said near me, though not to me, "My daughter sat for a portrait lately for an artist in town. Witherspoon by name; it's brilliant."

I interrupted delicately, clearing my throat to make both men turn toward me. How exposed I felt but somehow managed to say in spite of it, "I do love art. Could I see your gallery, sir?"

Judge Bonds' chestnut cheeks shone when he smiled. "Pride's a sin, and I'm proud as sin of it—take that hall, right at the end."

Thanking him, I slipped away. The narrow corridor wound a bit, and at first I thought I might be lost. I passed a formal dining room, the kitchen, then finally spilled into an almost-quiet parlor.

It was tastefully baroque and haunted. Not by spirits, but by Nathaniel Witherspoon's hand. I didn't have to read a single plate to know which painting was his.

Ethereal, the colors swirled like summer clouds. I reached out to touch, because I thought I might actually dip my fingers into the fountain. That I could rub the silken hem of her dress and smell the geraniums there.

He'd captured life in paint. He'd captured *life*.

A strange sensation came over me, like embers blown across my skin. It was madness, but I turned. I ran down the hall, my heavy gown hissing on the polished floors, and I clutched a pillar to look out at the crowd.

They seemed like multitudes, hundreds of eyes, a symphony of laughter, but I looked for only one. He was there; he burned like a tattoo, I only had to find him. I cut between bodies, thoughtless as I skimmed past the backs of stranger gentlemen.

Pressed against a rail, I caught my breath. All the lights had gone gold. And there danced Zora, lilies on her shoulders, with Thomas Rea. His hand pressed into her waist, wickedly possessive, and I saw her slip closer to him.

Revelation sizzled on my shoulders—it was the truth. I'd foreseen the truth! Though I'd done nothing but see, I felt wonderfully responsible. As if this moment had come to pass because of me, and I was proud! They were so beautiful together. My fingers fluttered against my throat, and I turned to find someplace quiet. And I wasn't surprised at all when I raised my eyes and looked right into Nathaniel's.

Offering my hand, I said, "There you are."

"I didn't mean to keep you waiting."

My dance card dangled from my wrist; he brushed the ribbon aside to kiss me there. Then he drew me to the floor, and the crowd dissolved. They could have danced in London, for as distant as they seemed. Nathaniel took one hand and rested his other on my waist, branding me deliciously.

We moved, somehow elemental. I felt like fire, the skies poured rain that rattled on the roof, the earth wavered to teach us the steps of this dance, and like air we floated across the floor together. We were all four points on the map, turning and turning like a compass.

Lifting my chin, I tried to stay safe in the darkness of his gaze. "I saw your painting."

Nathaniel smiled. "Did you like it?"

"No," I said, and then when his proud face fell, I hurried to say, "I wanted to step into it."

Squeezing my hand, he tipped me back and said, "You should see the good ones."

How naked I felt then, all my neck exposed, my chest too, down to the swell my corset made of my bust. Breath caught in my throat, I straightened and said, "I'm not sure I would survive the good ones."

The stars could have burned out around us, the moon

could have fallen from the sky, and I wouldn't have known it. Not when he leaned indecently close and pressed his cheek against mine to murmur, "Tell me a secret."

I wanted him to tell me how he stopped time like that. How he read my mind. I wanted to admit I wondered if thoughts of me troubled him when he lay awake at night. But I could make none of that come to my lips. They seemed too much, like I had given myself up to ruination on purpose.

Instead, still flush with my victory, I whispered back, "I've seen the future."

He didn't laugh. He didn't mock, not like he had done at Privalovna's performance. In the middle of our waltz, he stopped, nose to nose with me. He uncovered me with a look that somehow bared him, too.

And his question told me everything—that he stopped time because he needed me, that he read my mind because we were one. That I troubled his nights, indeed, because what he asked revealed all.

"Am I with you there?"

After the dance, Zora and I ran to stand beneath the brick *cochère,* waiting for a cab to come around.

The rain had slackened, leaving the air cold and clean, and I took great, deep swallows. Nathaniel's cologne clung to my gown, and I selfishly kept it bound beneath my manteau.

"I will never be so happy again," Zora sang, ducking out to check the sky.

Playful, I tugged the ribbons of her coat. My dance was a secret, even to her. I shared my giddiness but nothing else. For the moment, it was mine alone. Nathaniel's hand in mine, his future in mine. In a moment, August's bald planning to lift himself up with a suitable marriage of mine had been dashed. Worst, or best, I didn't care at all!

I had too much joy in me to hide, even if I kept the reason of it to myself. Everything had aligned, and when Zora turned to me, I took her hands and made her dance with me.

"I say this is only the beginning." I lifted my chin and dared Zora to argue.

"You mad romantic," she said. "Come on, clumsy! Lead!"

So I led, and we laughed, dancing into the night. My sunset vision hadn't been a spark—it was a forging. We'd been made new in it. How earnestly I thought magic would carry us through.

My name whispered woke me from my dreams.

I felt pulled on strings, my body lifted up before my mind thought to command it. Smoothing my hands across the coverlet, I nudged Zora. She sighed, tugging tighter into herself. A cool touch shimmered across my throat and then another, and that's what truly woke me.

Turning toward the cold, I found the window open. Not entirely, just an inch. Enough to let dangerous night air creep in. Covers thrown aside, I padded to the window to close it. Just as I reached for the sash, a shadow crossed the yard.

Indistinct of form and shape, it moved so fast that at first I doubted I had seen anything at all. I pulled the window shut, leaning as close to the glass as I could manage without fogging it.

I watched. I waited.

Then it came again, quick and black as a raven, but ever so much bigger that I thrilled to see it. It passed above the ground, but well below my window, a specter in reverse shades. Beneath my skin, I felt a familiar turning—the heat of being watched unawares.

Slipping into my robe, I hurried downstairs. I heard Mrs. Stewart working in the kitchen, but I didn't slow on my way to the back door. If she heard it open, she'd think only that

I meant to use the privy. Certainly, I intended to walk that way.

"Is anyone there?" I asked, shuddering when I stepped into the rain-scrubbed dark. It struck me then that I'd taken a fool's errand to come out on whim alone. My wrap could scarcely protect me from the gripping wind. Wet, frigid earth poured cold into my bones, my punishment for forgetting my slippers.

Yellow lights flickered into the alley. When I stopped, I heard people talking. Laughing. Their voices echoed into the alley, spilling out of houses indeterminate. Their lives turned in motion, they spoke freely, entirely unaware of my presence.

If I wanted to, I could eat my fill of their secrets—banal secrets, though. A woman to the left wondered aloud where her iron was. A man to the right exclaimed that the gas taps poisoned us all in our sleep.

Amelia, the wind breathed, fingering through my hair and slipping into my robe. Night turned almost physical around me, taking liberties, murmuring confidences, binding me in dark and starry arms. When I leaned into it, the spice of Nathaniel's bay rum swirled around me.

He whispered into me, rich and real: *Amelia, Amelia.*

"Amelia!"

Mrs. Stewart broke my reverie with a sharp call. The cold slapped my hot cheeks. Bad enough that I kept giving myself over to fantasy; I'd come to imagine dark suitors where none were. Shamelessly put myself in his arms again, no regard to propriety—my mind ran wicked and headlong before me, oh!

How long had I been out in the dark? How long had I pressed myself against the alley fence? Snatching two sticks of wood from the pile by the privy, I hurried back to the house. I ran on the golden carpet laid by light spilling from the door.

"I took a fright," I told her, dumping tinder in the firebox just inside.

"You'll take your death," Mrs. Stewart replied, and closed the night outside, where it belonged.

Nine

ALL ENCHANTMENT HAD TO FADE, and for us it faded by morning light. Sunday was worship, and come Monday morning we returned to our chilly classroom. Thomas made no appearance at all, which distracted Zora entirely. And my mind strayed far from reciting, off to a row house in Mount Vernon Place—a destination I could only imagine.

Twice I had to offer my knuckles for rapping, which delighted the littlest students beyond all telling of it. My pleasure in taking classes dimmed considerably. When Miss Burnside released us to our lunch pails, Zora and I shivered in a corner of the school's yard. A lattice arch stood in the middle, quite handsome in summer, no doubt.

The old vines of climbing flowers clung to the sides, and its bench seat swayed alluringly. But it was not yet summer — in cool, gusty spring, the arch wobbled and threatened, and we hurried to stay as far from it as we could.

"You're armored," Zora teased. "Protect me from it."

I made a face at her and stole the apple from her lunch pail. That was all the answer she deserved.

Edwina Polk minced toward us. It wasn't an unkindness to describe her this way—she was a tiny thing, no bigger than my thumb, it seemed. And all her gowns cut close to her ankles. She had no choice but to take hobbled steps, which made her seem both fashionable and pitiable at once.

"Did you just adore the petit fours at Judge Bonds' dance?" she asked. "I wasn't invited, but I heard everything was delicious."

Zora said, "I don't think I had a single one, to tell the truth."

"She was too busy waltzing with Thomas." I crunched my purloined apple, savoring the tart sweetness across my tongue.

"Which," Zora announced loftily, "Amelia entirely predicted."

Shock clasped me tight; I couldn't believe she'd said it so plainly. Before I could protest or perhaps pull my bosom friend's ear until she came to her senses, Edwina leaned in breathlessly.

She bumped my hip with hers, shoving me down forcibly so she could share our bench. "A prediction? Really?"

"No—" I started.

"Yes!" Zora lit from the inside—a color besides chapping cold in her cheeks. "It's brilliant, actually. Amelia's so modest, I hate to embarrass her. But her very first night in Baltimore, she had a vision of me dancing with Thomas Rea in a new dress, and Saturday night it came true."

My throat tightened, and I managed to squeak, "It was more a daydream . . ."

"Do you think you could tell my fortune?" Edwina asked.

"It's a very private thing," Zora said.

No, I should say she prevaricated entirely. I had not the first idea where she got these notions or how she came to say them with such authority, but she continued on apace. "Of course, she'd love to do it, but it's so taxing—we really can't risk it for diversion's sake. You understand."

Disappointment furrowed Edwina's ginger brow. Strumming her fingers on the curve of her lunch pail, she summoned a nearly perfect look of dissatisfied agreement. "Of course." Then, struggling to find another entrance to conversation, she asked, "Have you seen the Mysterious Privalovna yet?"

Patting her hand, I murmured, "Yes. She's a bit of a fraud, I'm afraid."

"Ugh," Edwina said. She dropped her pail at her feet and turned to us. "Why is everything interesting just out of our reach?"

Zora cast off her playfulness, leaning past me to ask, "Edwina, what's the matter with you?"

For a moment, Edwina swore there was nothing the matter. After all, the weather was turning, and she would have a new lawn promenade gown soon. With brown velvet ribbon, even, the screaming height of design. But Zora plucked at her, until Edwina cast her eyes down and offered a soft confession.

"I'm entirely restless lately," she said. I let her take a bite of my apple and watched her face transform as she chose her words. "I've never been anywhere, did you know that? I've never done anything daring. I've never misbehaved."

A warm rush of familiarity filled me. She could be describing my life, up until the very moment I set foot on the docks in the distance. Though I knew in my heart I should be spending my city time learning to be a proper lady who would be an admirable and gentle wife, I couldn't quite bring myself to recommend it. "So let's misbehave a bit. I'm a bit of an expert in getting sent home from school. Would you like to start there?"

"Oh, no," Edwina said, leaning away from me. "I couldn't."

"You just said you wanted to," Zora pointed out.

"My father would—"

Dismissing him with a wave, Zora said, "Dash your father."

Suddenly, Edwina went quite scarlet. "Zora Stewart, honestly!"

"You don't have to be a paragon yet," I suggested, but I already knew that Zora's filthy mouth had ended this conversation.

Sniffing, Edwina gathered her lunch pail. "But I should try, at least!"

We watched her totter away, and when she was out of earshot, I turned to Zora. "You're the most maddening puzzle. Half the time I want to be good like you, and half the time you're so wicked, I don't know what to do."

"That's easy." Zora tugged one of my hair ribbons loose

and hopped up to bid me chase. "Be like me all the time, half-good and half-wicked! It will save you ever so much trouble."

I chased her—of course I did. She was bright as any star, and no matter what I was meant to do in Baltimore, I, instead, found myself plotting a course between Zora and Nathaniel, duty abandoned for destiny—setting free the little wildness that grew in my heart. We laughed at the cold and daringly ducked the lattice, playing as the children in short skirts and unbound hair did. As if we had no care in the world.

And I suppose at that moment, we didn't.

❀ ❀ ❀

"So he said, 'Add me to your card.'" Zora tipped the china pot to refresh her cup of tea.

"And Zora said," I cut in, reaching for the milk, "'My reels are spoken for.'"

A mindful hostess, Zora turned to refresh my cup, too, which had the advantage of offering a dramatic pause before she finished the story again. "Then he looked at me just so and replied, 'I'm asking for the waltzes. All of them.'"

Nearly upending the sugar bowl, Mattie clapped her hands on the edge of the table. "Sweet charity, tell it again, Zora!"

Spooning milk through my tea, I laughed and laughed. Mattie had spent much of the dance in repairs of a torn hem. So, like me, she'd missed the brilliant storming of Zora's dance card by one Mr. Thomas Rea, Division Street.

That's how his calling card read, the one he left in our foyer this morning, inscribed with a handwritten *p.r.* on the back—*pour remercier,* for thanks—for Zora, who'd bewitched him 'til the last of the night.

Playing at a swoon, Sarah batted her lashes and chirped, "'I'm asking for the waltzes.'"

"'All of them,'" I intoned.

Zora bubbled with laughter. "Stop it!"

"How can you ask that of us?" Snapping her fan open, Sarah fluttered it wildly. "This is the most exciting thing that's happened to any of us. I want to live it again and again."

"Well, you know there's always the public dance in Annapolis," Mattie said.

Tea raised to her lips, Sarah stopped before sipping and said, "That's too long a drive if we can't stay the night."

"It's too long a drive without guarantee," Zora agreed. She squeezed the delicate sugar tongs between her fingers, making the silver tick with each compression. "Amelia, tell our fortunes before we resign ourselves to a week-end with cousin Agnes."

A groan went round the table, three voices joined in mutual distress. Quite surprised to be put in a spotlight so suddenly, I looked at them with a helpless smile. "What do you expect me to tell you?"

Zora waved the tongs. "Wondrous things, like last time!"

She was a shameless thing, so I leveled my cup and remarked, "But, Miss Stewart, it's so taxing."

With a distinctly unladylike snort, Zora gave me a poke. "These are our friends. Tax yourself for our entertainment. Just this once."

"I only saw a dress," I demurred. A sting crossed the back of my neck, and I tried to burn it off with a deep swallow of hot tea. "And a dance. I didn't mean to. It only happened that once."

Too excited now to consider tea or sandwiches, Mattie turned in her chair to offer her hands, to implore me. "Oh, it would be ever so lovely if you tried again!"

Sarah murmured something under her breath, and though I didn't catch it, I noted that it held a hint of derision. It struck a sour note in me, for whispering was rude and deliberately getting caught in a whisper ruder still. Ensuring that the subject of your gossip knew of your disdain was the height of it—even I knew that, country girl that I was.

So despite telling Edwina there was no diversion to be had in my prophesying, I turned to Mattie and squeezed her hands. "For you, I'll try."

※ ※ ※

Expectant eyes on me, I sat stiffly on a chair in the parlor, taking exaggerated breaths to calm myself. Being watched had the queerest effect—though they expected hysterics, I found myself too embarrassed to provide them.

Shifting my weight from side to side, I folded my hands and unfolded them. I leaned my head back and rolled it all around, but all that came to me was a thin and nervous giggle.

"It's so quiet," I said, then winced with laughter when Mattie jumped. "Beg your pardon."

Sarah held her tight smile, leaning forward to look at Mattie. "Boo, you little mouse."

"I have a nervous constitution. Everyone says so."

"It's all right," Zora said, intervening. She stood up in a

flurry of skirts, holding her hands out. "It was a valiant effort, but, alas, our cousin had one sending in her and it was for me. Weep if you must. Try not to hate me!"

As Zora moved to put the room right again, I pulled my chair closer to Mattie's to comfort her. "I'm sure whatever you wanted me to see will come true."

"I didn't know what I wanted," Mattie admitted. So pale, so dear — I wanted to fold her right up and carry her in my pocket, where none of the ugly world could trouble her.

I thought to have a word with Sarah later, for while I appreciated boldness in doses, it was plain to anyone that Mattie did not. Sharp manners and looks only enhanced the tremulousness of her nature, and I thought Sarah's way with her bordered on cruel.

Even now she snapped her fan open and closed, a drumming very like fingers on a board in its repetition. With each furling, Mattie started, little quakes that never entirely subsided, though she knew the source of the sound.

Passing behind her, Zora said lightly, "Then you go away satisfied, don't you?"

"I suppose I do."

Velvet and brocade crackled as Zora threw open the curtains. We all three raised our hands, little moles suddenly exposed to the sky. A shot of liquid gold tore through my fingers.

A reverie came fast over me, sunset's glimmering light spilling a stage before me. A swirl of fireflies coalesced into Sarah's form—it had to be her, for she alone had a gown just for archery. Only *she* pulled back a bowstring with that much accomplishment.

I felt myself rising up, my hands skimming the air to mirror the pull. Closer I came to this gilded image of our sunswept cousin, until I found myself looking through her eyes. No small amount of pleasure expanded when we took our breath, turned with perfect poise toward the target.

A whip cracked. We dropped to our knees. The crescent shape of the bow quivered as it fell on the remains of a flawed arrow. We pressed our hands to our face. In dusk-drenched gold, there was beauty in the blood that poured through our gloved fingers.

Our admiration breathed once and died when the pain spilled forth after it. A raw, savage agony filled our head. Sobbing, we fell into the cool grass. The sudden, ugly scent of sal volatile burned beneath my nose, and I thrashed.

Gilt gardens melted to the rich mulberry shades of the

Stewarts' parlor. Raising my hand to my nose, I cringed away. Three pairs of ravenous, waiting eyes followed me as I tried to find my feet.

"You went insensible; it was amazing," Sarah said, hauling me up on one side.

On the other arm, Mattie asked, "Did you see something for me?"

Trying to find a steady center once more, I freed myself from their grips. Murmuring my thanks, I smoothed my gown and backed away from them. A horrifying pain pressed behind my eye. I wanted to cry.

The first sending had come so sweetly. The message had been so dear that I was happy to carry it. But even as I looked on Sarah and her haughty carriage, I couldn't stand the thought that my own bias had wished an ill sight on me.

She wasn't terrible—she had nothing but kindness for me, and Mattie didn't seem to mind her pecking. Even if she did, no one would deserve such a punishment.

Zora capped the salts, leaving them on the mantel to come to my side. Arms wrapped around me, she murmured, gently reassuring, "I think she swooned, that's all. Too much tea, not enough sandwich."

"Corset's too tight," I agreed.

A bitter guilt overwhelmed me. What if those things I saw were not my heart's desire, but the truth? I owed it to Sarah to warn her against tragedy.

My cheek still stung with the phantom strike, and when I looked on her round face, I saw exactly the course the wound would cross—through her dark, arched brow, across the round of her cheek.

Taken by vertigo, I trembled when I realized that such a wound would sacrifice one of her pretty brown eyes.

I clutched Zora's arm for support and said, "Mind your arrows, Sarah, I beg you."

And then I flung myself toward the kitchen, to be sick in private.

❀ ❀ ❀

Sitting with a basin in her lap, Mrs. Stewart waited for us to twist the eyes from potatoes, then took them to peel. With her apron pinned just so and a cloth draped across her gown, she seemed rather like a nurse.

Well, except that she was missing a white hat and a pocket full of sweets. Oh, and she scolded us instead of petting us, yet again.

• 129 •

"Keeping up this state of high dudgeon plays havoc on a girl's constitution," she said, her knife flashing. "Modern or not, I'm raising ladies here."

Zora kept her eyes down, for I could see that at any moment she might burst out laughing. As I was the one to blame for most of the dudgeon in question, I hardly had room to find delight in the resulting havoc.

"It wouldn't do you a spot of harm to summer in Maine," Mrs. Stewart added. She gently kicked the foot of Zora's chair, reminding her to attend to her posture.

Zora shook a potato at her mother. "Would you risk my going wild just to make a point?"

"I would forget you're all but seventeen and tan your hide!"

For that, I did laugh. I troubled to bury in my hand, pretending to cough. I thought Zora might have a saucy reply, but if she did, a knock at the door cut her off.

The Stewarts only had a downstairs girl on Tuesdays and Thursdays, so Zora jumped to her feet to play the part. After all, there was the odd chance that Thomas might take leave of his senses and drop off another card for her on a day when he'd already left one.

"Sit, you," Mrs. Stewart said, handing off the basin and leaving her lap cloth in the chair to answer it herself. One never knew, and she could hardly risk our reputations by letting us loll at the door, talking to boys before dinner.

Moments later when we heard Thomas' voice, Zora and I nearly broke a neck apiece in our attempt to get to the hallway.

Thomas stood in the foyer, hat in hand—proved tall by comparison to the door behind him. Something troubled him, though. His shoulders curled like they had when Miss Burnside remonstrated him. My heart sank. I prayed there would be no trouble between him and Zora—no obstacle put there, either.

Zora pressed her face against my arm, like she had to gather strength just to put eyes on him. Her breath slipped hot through my sleeve as she whispered, "I take one look, and I want to run away with him."

"Where would you go?"

A warm light came on in Zora's eyes. "Anywhere. Anywhere at all. I shouldn't care if it were Shanghai."

When Thomas turned to leave, I shook Zora and spun her to at least look on him before he went. Across Mrs. Stewart's shoulder, they caught a glimpse and clung to that breathless moment for the little time it lasted.

Then the door closed, and Zora and I scrambled back to the kitchen. We were so clever and graceful in our return that we knocked over Mrs. Stewart's chair and lost three potatoes. With no time to retrieve them, we simply acted as though they belonged there when Mrs. Stewart returned.

"Who was that?" I asked innocently.

Mrs. Stewart put her foot on top of a potato, rolling it beneath her shoe. "I think you know."

Picking up the thread I'd stitched, Zora asked, "Was he on business, Mama?"

"You might say."

One by one, Mrs. Stewart snatched potatoes off the floor; our displays of cheek no longer amused her.

As the mood in the kitchen darkened considerably, Zora and I rededicated ourselves to our chore. Never had anyone found rubbing the eyes from potatoes so arduous and exacting work, the way we did while waiting for Mrs. Stewart to speak.

She passed my chair to retrieve hers. When she did, I saw an envelope in her hand—paper of the finest sort, closed with a seal of verdigris green. Would that I could see through parchment!

Mrs. Stewart sat, stiff and formal. "Let it not be said that I came into this agreement to keep you, Amelia, with blinders. I expected a measure of frivolity. I was young once. I anticipated the delights you'd both find in taking license."

My hands stilled.

"Convention may stifle, but it protects young women from their foolish whims."

"Mama," Zora dared, then shut up on receipt of a hard look.

Fanning herself in the heat of the kitchen, Mrs. Stewart became mortal again as she sighed. "You have good natures, and it's man's nature to take advantage of that. There's no boy who ever walked this earth with only selfless intention."

"What about the Lord?" Zora mumbled.

Mrs. Stewart squinted at her. "Do you really wish me to nip your bud, Zora Pauline?"

For me, I wished that this dreadful conversation would fade away. It was clear. The postmaster had mentioned my visit. Or Thomas himself felt honor-bound to report how closely I had danced with Nathaniel. God save me, perhaps both. I swallowed back a sour taste and trembled.

"Against my best judgment," Mrs. Stewart said, producing the letter, "this shall be the first, and only, time I acknowledge attentions made toward either of you out of turn."

Zora swelled in anticipation of taking it. Surprise plucked her brows when Mrs. Stewart instead delivered it to me.

"Wills is a fine boy who knows better," Mrs. Stewart said, reaching for the basin and her knife again. "I bade Thomas tell him he would carry no more entreaties. He can leave his card of a morning, the same as any other caller."

Confusion broke the tensioned air. I hadn't been found out, and apparently I had been called out for a total mystery. Why would Wills go to such trouble for me? We had barely met, and all that stirred me was his fine taste in papers.

Disappointed, Zora tossed a potato in the basin and reached for another. "What's that great auk have to say for himself?" She stared pointedly until I unfolded the letter.

"'Dear Miss van den Broek, forgive me for being so bold, but I've never enjoyed a dance so much as I did the one at Judge Bonds','" I read, a blush starting to light on my skin. "'If it pleases you and Miss Stewart, Mr. Rea and I shall number ourselves among those attending the public ball held by the Sons of Apollo in Annapolis, date and time listed below. The cause is the arts, and I appeal to the philanthropic nature so inborn in ladies of your stature, to humbly beg your kind consideration, should there be none other engagement of previous obligation on this occasion.'"

Mrs. Stewart said to no one in particular, "Fancy that. Who knew Wills could pen such a pretty letter?"

I shuffled the pages, and a sharp breath caught in my chest when I found not a closing, but an epigraph, written in a fine hand in the middle of the page. At once, the richness of bay rum cologne rushed up to torment me, stirred into the ink.

"And he signs his name, that's all," I lied, stuffing them into my polonaise. The letter needed no signature for me to understand. Thomas would no doubt attend the Sons of Apollo ball, but I would not find Wills there in search of me.

"Please, Mama," Zora said, already begging.

Whatever Mrs. Stewart's answer, I didn't hear it. Her voice drifted away from me—Zora's, too. I heard nothing but the echo of my own name. Pressing my hand to my breast, to the letter safely tucked away, I burned knowing how the letter truly ended.

> *Was it enough to wear the night with me just once,*
> *Amelia? I am unsatisfied.*
>
> > *Yours, obediently—*
> > *Nathaniel Witherspoon*

✺

Oakhaven

Broken Tooth, Maine

Autumn 1889

✺

Ten

"HAS SHE BEEN at that window all day?" August asked when he came in.

He brought autumn with him, a crisp scent of dried leaves and fires burned down in the village. Once the scent of wood smoke had delighted me, but no longer. Now it brought a low, slow throbbing to my brow.

Lizzy deflected the question. "She went out and picked morels this morning."

"She's gone mad," I said, stretching my arm across the windowsill, "not deaf."

The floor shook beneath August's boots. Bending down, he came so very close that I could see nothing but the reflection of my eyes in his. Catching my chin, he refused to let me look away. "I'm quite determined to put you straight, Amelia."

Forcibly, I broke his gaze and applied myself to the study of the seasons again.

Funny how our trees usually burst out in shades of flame come fall, but this year they had nothing but endless shades of dun and dark. I wondered if some tragedy had stolen all their colors, too.

"So they're not enough for stew," Lizzy said, picking up her thought as easily as she picked up her next stitch. "But perhaps dressing, if we've got any oysters. Or maybe you could bring some home tomorrow, Gus."

"What difference does it make," August asked, the question trailing behind him down the hall, "if she refuses to eat dressing or refuses to eat stew? I should like stew myself. It's my house, isn't it?"

"Spoiled," Lizzy murmured, an indulgent tone meant to curry my agreement, but I had no answer.

Every day felt like drowning to me. I woke and took a single, useless breath, then sank into the deep again. Every shape was shadows; every flavor, dust. What did it matter if I spent my days at the window or beneath the ground? I'd still destroyed Zora. I'd still burned Baltimore to the ground.

In the end, it was all the same.

Except the wonderful detonations that came when I crossed August. He shouted from his study, and soon thereafter he carried his storm back to the kitchen.

"What is this?" he demanded, slapping papers on the table. He raised his voice when I failed to raise my head. "I will have an explanation, and I will have it now!"

Reaching for one of the sheets that had drifted to the floor, Lizzy kept silent as she read. I traced her figure in the glass, the tips of my fingers marking the pretty curve of her cheeks as they turned from blush to ash.

August tapped a finger against the page. "Now you see, Elizabeth. Now you see, don't you?"

"That's enough," Lizzy murmured. But she folded the paper in half and fed it to the old iron stove. At once, she gathered her sewing and swept from the kitchen. For all the effort it took me to look after her, I only managed to see the hem of her skirt disappear around the corner.

I slipped my fingers in my hair, twisting and twisting at the braids looped there. "Oh, Gus, for shame. Look what you've done."

"Burn them all," he told me. And then, admirably, he went after his wife.

I didn't leave the chair so much as slip from it. Unboned and weak-muscled, I melted across the floor and came to sit against the wall. When I strained, I caught a few scattered pages. Straightening them in my lap to consider, I sighed. My handwriting drifted in a slope across the page.

Today in the vespers, I hear two boys drowning when the current calls them to sea.

Today in the vespers, I see a physician with winding cloths walking to the pastor's house.

Today in the vespers, I'm blind. I taste blood in my mouth, and I know not whose it is.

The smoke smelled no sweeter when it was premonitions burned. The paper turned to white ash before collapsing into the flames. Page after page, I destroyed, and I could well imagine the one Lizzy burned first:

Today in the vespers, I see my brother's wife, weeping tears and milk for the stillborn babe they put in the ground.

✳

Kestrels

Baltimore, Maryland

Summer 1889

✳

Eleven

"SHOULD YOU WISH to continue classes throughout the summer," Miss Burnside said, sweeping down the rows between our desks. "Please ask that your parents engage me before the last of the month to guarantee placement."

In spite of the kind offer, I felt quite certain that Zora and I would be spending our days in teas and callings instead of lessons. Summer broke over the city in the most pleasing way.

The harbor, for the moment, settled the heat to a suggestion. It gave us a season warm enough to go about without a wrapper, wearing light *chinoise* gowns instead of heavy brocade. It gave us a barbecue season to parade in the park and make eyes at any who pleased us.

Miss Burnside moved through the room as a barge through the harbor. She touched students to promote them to their next grade. Out of spite, she started at the last chair and worked her way forward.

"Give way," Zora mouthed to me.

Sitting as I did between her and Thomas, I had to tip back so they could exchange looks. It had become so regular that I was once tempted to fail an exam, just to let Thomas win my seat. My pride overwhelmed temptation, however, so I spent a good deal of time trailing my ribbons on the desk behind me so they could moon.

"Thank you, Miss Harrison; I shall see you again to begin sixth-form lessons," Miss Burnside sang behind me.

"Has your mother talked to Mrs. Castillo?" Thomas asked.

Zora leaned into the aisle to whisper back, "She sent a letter with Papa, and he'll return tomorrow with the answer, I expect. But she's never said no before now—like as not, she'll agree this time, too."

With a smile, I pointed out between them, "She only had to take three of you before. You've got an extra this year."

"Three, four, what's the difference?" Zora asked, and we all corrected our posture when Miss Burnside cracked her stick on a desk behind us.

"I'm sorry to say you'll need to repeat your fourth term," Miss Burnside told little Joey Dobbs.

When Miss Burnside drifted to the other side of the room, I craned back again.

Arms curled on the desk, Zora told Thomas, "In any case, it shouldn't matter. If we must, Sarah and Mattie could stay with Sarah's aunt. We'll prevail upon Mrs. Castillo's good nature to take the two of us."

"Where will you stay?" I asked, then colored for my shamelessness. Of the myriad of things not meant for young ladies to contemplate, a bachelor's sleeping arrangements was chief among them.

And, alas, it was not so much that I cared to know Thomas' particulars, but that I hoped he would divulge Nathaniel's in the telling.

"I thought to ride back that night," Thomas said, though that sounded entirely unlikely to me.

To Zora as well, for she hummed a note that called him a liar. Then, as if her trickery would go unnoticed, she asked, "Did Dr. Rea buy another horse of late?"

"He didn't," Thomas said, rising in his seat, bemused. "I planned to borrow one."

"And ride it hard on, thirty miles in the morning, then thirty more after the ball?" Clicking her tongue against her teeth, Zora sighed. "Poor borrowed beast."

Reaching across to my desk, Thomas tapped his finger on the edge of it. "Mind yourself, and let me save your country friend from herself."

"Oh, noble Mr. Rea," Zora teased, then jerked upright when Miss Burnside rapped her across the shoulders.

The willow stick was not thick enough to wreak damage, but it hurt. Not that any would know it from Zora's reaction. She bit her lips, swallowing laughter as desperately as ginger water on a hot day.

"I'm happy," Miss Burnside said, her teeth gritted in such a way that we could hardly believe her happy at all, "to graduate you, Miss Stewart. I wish you all the best at the new girls' High School next year."

Zora took to her feet and dipped low in an exquisite court bow. As we had no royalty in Baltimore, Zora's audacity astounded me, truly. "I am ever humbly in your debt, good lady Burnside."

Miss Burnside's expression never changed. But, oh, there was so much motion in that nothing. In a frosted silence, she waited for Zora to walk away before passing my desk. Everyone knew my half season of school was the end of my schooling entirely.

It would be quite rude to say outright that I should hurry off now to find a respectable man to keep me — ruder still for Miss Burnside to point out that she thought that as likely as my learning to fly. But she had to graduate me in some way, so she lit her fingers on my shoulder and said, "Good luck to you in all your endeavors, Miss van den Broek."

"Thank you," I murmured, and slipped away without further incident.

※ ※ ※

Of all the souls I thought *might* run down the street at us, I never expected Mattie Corey.

Yet there she came, skirts in one hand, her bonnet pressed flat with the other. Her lips parted and closed, and it looked like she called to us, though no sound came out. The running, it seemed, was the full extent of her ability to be ill-mannered.

"What's the matter?" Zora asked, very nearly pulled down when Mattie tipped and lost her balance before her.

Thomas held out hands to catch them, tipping them both aright with a single, subtle push.

And then he stood a little straighter—perhaps pride for his gallantry, but more likely to prove his propriety. No one would claim he was prissy, but he clung, with weary determination, to etiquette when we let him.

"Amelia's vision," Mattie said breathlessly, slapping at her mint batiste suit. She hurried to smooth herself. "It's true—it came true! You saved her, Amelia."

"How do you mean?" I asked, stunned once that she claimed it true—stunned twice that there was any saving to be had.

Mattie slipped her arm into mine, pulling me down the street. "This morning at practice, one of Sarah's arrows exploded as she drew!"

Coming around to Mattie's other elbow, Zora exclaimed, "Exploded?"

"Right as I'm standing here," Mattie said, nodding. Stopping abruptly in the street, she leaned back, lifting her chin as if she carried a bow. "She nocked it, and just at full draw, we heard an awful crack. Awful! I screamed!"

A crack of knuckles could make Mattie scream, so that hardly set the scene. But a quivering ran beneath my skin as I squeezed her arm. "And it broke?"

"Exploded! Sarah threw her hands up at the last moment—look!" From her pocket, Mattie produced several

wicked shards, one with a tattered bit of feather still clinging to it.

Reaching to take one, I raised it to my face. Between
blinks, I saw the golden specter of my vision again. I felt the
agony across my face, the steaming splash of blood . . .

Shaking my head to clear it, I asked Mattie, "And no
harm came to her?"

"You saved her," Mattie said, warm with reverence.

I should have been awed, or humbled, or afraid. A tragedy had been avoided, by whatever means! I should've
bowed my head to give thanks or fallen to my knees in joy
that our cousin was well—and I *was* happy! But coloring it
all was my own awful sense of accomplishment.

They'd begged me to draw forth a vision—and I had.

❀ ❀ ❀

On our first day free after classes, Zora and I headed into
town proper. Smoke curled its fingers across a pure blue
sky, but the wind kindly took the scent of a hot day out to
the Chesapeake.

"Have care," Zora said, as she backed away at the print
shop. "I'm peeking in next door."

I waved her off, for what did it matter if we stood

together waiting for my calling cards or if I stood on my own? A string of bells jangled overhead as I went inside after my own errand.

"Order for Amelia van den Broek?" I asked the wiry man at the counter.

"Hold there, miss." He ducked into the back.

I occupied myself browsing, for the engraver kept samples of his work everywhere. Every so often, I flicked a look at the door, not entirely anxious to be alone, but wishing Zora would hurry at least. Firmly, I chastened myself, for truthfully, she'd gone on *my* errand.

One of Zora's New York aunts had sent a recent issue of *The Delineator*, full of lovely swirled and curled hairstyles to imitate. We found a Grecian sweep of curls, double-bound with ribbon, which we decided would suit Zora especially well.

"Silver," I hoped, to twinkle against the chestnut waves of her hair. She'd probably come back with lapis or sapphire. Zora had her favorites, and no one could sway her once she'd fixed an idea in her mind. The door swung open again, and I turned to tease her about more useless blue ribbon. But it wasn't Zora—in came Nathaniel, with a sure and certain gaze.

"Miss van den Broek," he said, dipping his head to acknowledge me.

Not once, never once, had I seen even the first hint that our chance encounters surprised him. Nor did his smooth face betray any effervescence in his veins. *My* blood turned to champagne whenever he came near.

"Mr. Witherspoon," I replied, and pressed myself to the counter.

Though now he stood behind me, I could make out his shape as keenly as if I saw it. Each step he took vibrated through me. Though he stopped at a charitable distance, his murmurs slipped into my ear, intimate as if he pressed his lips to my skin. "I hear glorious things about you."

My breath fled, and it took more than one attempt to find a reply. "I hear nothing about you at all."

"What would you wish to?" he asked.

Heat trailed from his flesh to mine, as he came to stand at the other end of the counter. Catching glimpses of him from the edge of my eye, the champagne in me spilled over. "Good news, if you have it."

"I think you shall see something glorious in the vespers," he said, tugging the fingertips of his glove to effect a slow, wicked appearance of his bare flesh. "Beneath Apollo's banner, a lady's gaze turned toward mine."

Gripping the edge of the counter, I whispered, "What are you on about?"

"Miss Holbrook's remarkable salvation, of course." He folded his gloves and turned toward me. "You really do see the future."

"You asked for my secret." I twisted my fingers together, trying not to drift into his gaze, but I did all the same.

Oh, terrible wonders, Nathaniel reached out, and I thought for a moment—I wantonly wished—that he meant to touch my face with his bare hand. Instead, he slipped his glove into my pocket. "Yes, I did, didn't I?"

His footsteps receded, his shadow left the edge of my gaze, but I heard no opening of the door. I thought about dashing after him, to see if I could catch him melting into the crowd. Suddenly, the bells above the door clamored as Zora returned in triumph.

"Two yards each silver and blue," she crowed.

I could only nod my approval as I slipped my hand into Nathaniel's glove.

We carried ourselves into the house in a whispering swirl of skirts and bonnets half-removed, apologizing gaily to the downstairs girl who came to meet us. We very nearly knocked her over, and I had to settle her with a pet on the shoulder.

"Yes, Molly?" Zora asked.

The downstairs girl offered up a box and a slightly pained expression. "Your callers, Miss Stewart, Miss van den Broek."

"Good God," Zora cursed in wonderment.

I took the box, shaking it and reaching inside to pull out not Thomas' single card, to which we had grown accustomed, but a handful. Exchanging a befuddled look with Zora, I asked, "Are these all new?"

"Did nothing but answer the door this morning," Molly said, her annoyance barely disguised.

Pushing herself from between us, she stalked back to the kitchen, her shoulders drawn nearly to her ears. I shouldn't have laughed at her ire, but I did keep it low and just for Zora's consumption at least.

"Let's see, then," Zora said, crowding against my shoulder.

I thumbed through the cards one by one. "That's yours," I said, handing off Thomas' card, then shuffled through the next several in quick succession. We had one from Mattie and Sarah each, several from school friends just to tell us they would be leaving for the summer—which we already knew from speaking to them at school, but nevertheless.

Most intriguing were the cards marked *p.p.—pour présenter.* We were two girls of no particularly wide circle, sought by none unfamiliar to us. What could have happened that suddenly we had six cards begging to meet us? Giddy and exhilarated, we took turns reading the names to each other.

"Oh, I know her," Zora said, stopping at a gaudy card of strawberry pink. It even had a color impression of strawberries at the top. This hideous delight stood out among the rest of the proper cards, all white or ecru, and Zora laughed as she held it up. "Of her, I mean. She's above us, not that you'd know it. Their fortune's in sugar, of all things."

"But what does she want?" I wondered aloud.

"To make our acquaintance," Zora said, stating the obvious. She shook the box to make sure there were no more cards in it, then waltzed away toward the kitchen. "Tomorrow we shall go calling to find out!"

But we had no need to wait. Just at the time for informal tea, Mattie and Sarah presented themselves at our doorstep—with a friend.

Twelve

I KNEW YOU WOULDN'T MIND," Sarah told us, one hand on her guest's back and the other out to squeeze mine. Turning to Zora, she imposed, warming her with a brash smile and, finally, an introduction. "This is Miss Nella Mfana; Nella, may I present Miss Zora Stewart and Miss Amelia van den Broek?"

"A pleasure," we murmured by turns, and I caught fluttering Mattie by the fingers, tugging her closer with a wink.

"And to what do we owe it?" Zora asked, pleasant but pointed. Of course, we should invite them in for tea, and no doubt we would, but it was strange providence, indeed, for anyone to arrive uninvited, much less without having left a card at the very least.

Sweeping us into the parlor, for Sarah had that commanding sort of presence, she spread out her hands imploringly. "Miss Mfana, if you would plead your case?"

"Oh, do hear her out," Mattie whispered to me, squeezing my hand.

Of course, I would, but I couldn't contain my concern at such intrigue. I could, no better than anyone, solve a case — and perhaps so much worse! Zora, at least, knew this city and its families — I didn't know anyone but her friends.

Though Nella was strongly built, her voice turned wispy as she admitted, almost shamefully, "There's a shade over my house, Miss van den Broek. My mother passed on two years gone, but though Papa and I have come out of mourning, it seems . . . I feel as though she's angry with us."

A chill teased the back of my neck, for I knew well that sensation. When the fever took my parents, I thought I should never be happy again . . . and I was ashamed at first when I found I *could* be. I felt like a callous wretch the day I packed my mourning clothes and uncovered the mirrors.

"I'm truly sorry for your loss, Miss Mfana," I said, taking her hands. "Would that I could ease your suffering, most assuredly I would."

Tears welled in Nella's eyes. "Mama's best cup fell from the mantel and shattered last night. Her wedding spoons have gone missing. A little drawing she kept over the stove burned right up! I'm afraid. I'm afraid of my own mother. Can you tell her she still means everything to me?"

Taken aback, I stiffened. I'd only caught future glimpses — it seemed another gift entirely to speak to the beyond. Beside me, Mattie whispered, something calming or encouraging — I wasn't sure which.

Oh, and how my heart ached, as I admitted, "That's no talent I possess, Miss Mfana. Sometimes I see things, but I have no spirit guides to carry my words."

"Does she come for me, then?" Nella asked plaintively. "Will she take me to the grave with her?"

Even Sarah gasped softly at such a horrid thought. But it was fair of Nella to beg it—it *was* a question my ability should be able to answer, if I could summon it.

Doubt etched at me. My sendings came unbidden. Zora hadn't asked, and Mattie's plea brought me a glimpse of Sarah's fate instead. And yet a streak of pride rose like flame. Yes, my gift was undisciplined and uncontrolled, but I *had* seen beyond. I didn't know what I might accomplish if I tried.

"Come with me to the window," I said, gesturing her that

way. "I can't promise you anything, but I can try. Zora, could you have the salts ready, if I need them?"

The parlor reverberated like a plucked string, some of us in motion, some of us still, but something like excitement stirring through us all.

Inwardly, I recounted how the first visions had come on — clearing myself of all thoughts because the noise had been so great, the direct flash of sunset in my eyes.

Brushing the curtain back, I squinted at the reddening streaks crossing the sky, then turned to Nella once more. "Think, very clearly, on your mother's face for me."

Nella's eyes darted away, then back at me. Conscious of being watched, she seemed to hesitate, but finally dropped her lashes. I put my hands in hers, then leaned my head against the window.

Though Lady Privalovna had proved to be a fraud, I still took from her the act of drawing in deeply, of exhaling. I felt it opened me in a way, unlidding me so I could be filled with gold.

As the sun sank, my thoughts drifted, as if I might fall asleep. But then a certain cut of light streaked before me. It ran through the streets like a river, filling the whole of the city with liquid amber, washing all away but the flickering, glimmering dance of stardust.

As the sparks flew up, the tableau before me changed. I stood in an unfamiliar chamber—a parlor much like the Stewarts', but unlike it all the same. Books lined one wall, and a pianoforte occupied the corner, a lace runner draped across its length.

When I turned to orient myself, I saw through Nella's eyes, her face in the glass above the mantel.

I'd become one with her. We took first one step, then another, to reveal the whole of our body. Though we had no colors but gilded ones, we gazed in certainty at the creamy shades of organza and lace at our shoulders. We had no doubt that the veil draped over our hair was white or very like it.

Reaching up, we touched a cameo at our throat, and, oh, the longing fondness that rushed through our breast when we did. It was a joyous peace, one of comfort, that we carried as we turned to meet a handsome man in a morning coat. When he leaned to kiss us, the vision melted as wax down a candle.

"Miss Mfana," I said, reaching uncertainly for my chair so I could sit.

A wavering daze clung to me, as if I had gone too long without a meal to fortify me. Still, I summoned myself and looked up at the girl who clasped her hands so tightly they trembled. "She's not angry. Wear her cameo when you wed, so she can celebrate with you."

The tremble that had started in Miss Mfana's hands spread to her shoulders and then throughout her, until she shook with tears. "I don't even have a beau."

Awash with my own power, I simply said, "You shall."

❊ ❊ ❊

Delighted with our new popularity, Zora and I took calls the whole week. Strangers and friends alike came to the Stewarts' door, and without fail we served them tea and fortunes. We accepted—quite guiltily—Edwina Polk in the very first days.

She sat nearest the stairs, pale and freckled with a cup tipped between her palms. Having her in the Stewarts' parlor disconcerted me. For the first time, I truly realized how much better-heeled she was than we.

Certainly my brother, August, had pretended we were wealthy, and the Stewarts were not impoverished by any standard. But Edwina's dress matched the illustrations in my latest *Harper's Bazar* magazine. Her gloves were so new, the fingers had not yet been worn smooth.

But there I sat with a strange measure of power over

her—for having answers to unknowable questions. When the light struck me that day, I shivered in the gilt veil and saw Edwina on the deck of a steamer ship. The ribbons in her hat trailed in the wind, and a handsome boy—a stranger entirely to me—came to take her elbow.

"It might be," I told her dizzily, as Zora threatened with the smelling salts, "a honeymoon tour, I think?"

Trembling, Edwina put the cup down hard. "Is he handsome?"

"Yes."

Zora swooped close again, but I batted the salts away as Edwina slid to the edge of her chair. Her gingery lashes fluttered as she grasped at her future, as if by knowing it, she could somehow steer it. "Did he say anything?"

"I'm sorry, I only see," I told her. Then I swore, "But he's tall and blond, I think. He seemed quite kind."

This stopped Edwina short. Slowly, she pulled a locket from inside her collar and opened it. She showed me a handsome portrait of a boy. He had a soft, thoughtful expression and hair the color of wheat. As if choosing her words with calipers, Edwina said, "Is this him?"

A crystalline chill took me, the way it had when I saw Zora's vision dress in her mother's real hands. My lips tingled as I touched the locket. "Yes. Yes, that's him! And you had a pale suit on, with a dark ribbon around here, that matched the one on your hat."

Calm came over Edwina, and she smiled. "Thank you," she said, closing the locket to drop it in her collar again. She kissed my cheek and Zora's too before she left.

She crossed our front walk satisfied, and I had to admit, it was a relief that most of my sendings were of this bland, happy variety. I saw one girl sketching the ruins in Athens. Another returned to Tokyo to summer with her grandmother.

With each innocuous vision, my confidence grew. I had it all nearly figured out—how to sit at the window, how to catch the light in my eyes just so. Where the gift came from remained a tantalizing mystery. I only knew that if I welcomed the sunset, the sunset would speak to me.

Awash in the intrigue of having so many call for us, Zora and I were careful not to get too drunk on it. It was a terrible challenge to mind ourselves, though, for it seemed no girl in Baltimore cared to go without her future told—not even the most privileged ones.

The sugar heiress sent her strawberry card again. It was, more or less, a summoning to her door.

Therefore, we found it quite funny that the butler seemed poised to turn us away. I suppose our lawn gowns weren't the most fashionable. What could little mice like us want with Miss Lawrence, after all?

But Zora raised her chin. "Sir, we will go away unannounced. So long as you realize you're turning away Maine's Own Mystic, Miss Amelia van den Broek."

How fortunate that I choked on my own laughter. Offering him more than a trembling smile might have ruined Zora's grand introduction. But what was brilliant was that the man actually paid her mind.

"One moment," he said, and disappeared. When he returned, he led us into the most richly appointed parlor I'd seen yet. I felt like I might meet the First Lady here, among the crystal and the lace.

Instead, I met a young woman adorned in layer upon layer of pink. Not one inch of her contrasted. Even her pale blond hair reflected the rose of her gown. She matched her cards well, for she looked like nothing more than a giant spring strawberry.

"I'd like to take tea at your house, and so I need a reassurance," she said, without preamble.

Smiling curiously, I looked to Zora, who said, "Pardon?"

"I've got a good many friends. I must be assured there's room enough for all of them in your parlor," Miss Lawrence said. She didn't bother to sit or offer tea. In fact, it seemed very much that she intended to flit away without even meeting our gazes straight on. "We're all very interested in having our futures told."

"Are you?" Zora said. Her voice had grown dangerous. Miss Lawrence had no idea how close to a lashing she was. I did, and I thought better of making enemies of an heiress, so I interjected.

"Right now I'm taking single guests. It's very . . . taxing to part the veil."

Zora swelled beside me. I didn't dare look at her, for no doubt her expression would send me into fits of giggles. But what could I do? Miss Lawrence had presented me with an absurd notion; it was only fair to give her one in return.

But instead of throwing us out, she finally sat! The ivory of her fan cracked in her hands as she looked me straight on. "I've never heard of a spiritualist admitting impediment."

My chest tightened. "Only a fraud can promise you everything. It's truth that has limits."

"I see." Something dawned on Miss Lawrence's face, something rather like realization. I couldn't imagine what thoughts distracted her so, but she cracked her fan again and said, "And I suppose each supplicant must pay for your visions."

"What? No!" I gathered myself. "If I see, I see freely."

Zora stepped hard on my foot, but I couldn't help the exclamation. However useless my gift might be most of the time . . . and all right, however wicked I might be sometimes, I was mostly a good girl. What kind of a good girl charged a fee for insight? I felt dirty just thinking of it.

Suspicious now, Miss Lawrence narrowed her eyes. "No one pays?"

"No one," I said, and dragged Zora closer to me. It was a strange call, and I meant to end it immediately. "My gift is free. It is singular. I make no promises; what comes to me comes. If you should wish me to look, then call at sunset."

Outside, Zora squeezed my hand and told me, "You can't speak to Helen Lawrence that way, you know!"

"I did and survived it," I said. And I laughed, because I expected that to be my first and last sitting with society.

How surprised I was to discover I was wrong.

Perhaps no one had been so curt before; maybe it was just that my gift was genuine. But a whole stream of society debutantes flowed through the Stewarts' parlor, dammed only when it came time for our week-end in

Annapolis. It was like Zora's joking announcement had come true.

I was Maine's Own Mystic, and I was in demand.

※ ※ ※

"I'm glad to see you go," Mrs. Stewart said, fussing with the luggage on the victoria.

Grabbing one end of a thick leather belt, she leaned back with all her weight to tighten it. Then, quickly, she closed the iron clasps to fix it in place. "You've done nothing but eat and drink us into the poorhouse."

Giggling, Zora twisted around, propping up to watch her. "You always said you would see me socially accomplished."

Mrs. Stewart offered an unladylike snort, then a grunt when she fixed the second strap. "That was before I had to resort to selling my hair combs for tea and cookies."

"I'm given to understand that there's a market for shorn hair as well."

"Oh, Zora," I said.

Cracking her umbrella against our trunk, Mrs. Stewart made a satisfied sound, then came to the sideboard of the carriage. She stepped up, clinging to the handle as she pulled Zora's wrapper closed. "I should thank you very much to leave that tongue at home. If you should embarrass us with Mrs. Castillo . . ."

"Mama!" Zora recoiled, incredulous. "I would never!"

"That goes for Amelia, too," Mrs. Stewart said. She tugged on my cloak's collar to check its fastener, then hopped down. "Whatever spiritualist nonsense you goslings have been up to lately, I expect none of it while you're in Annapolis."

My neck grew hot. "Yes, ma'am."

"It's not nonsense," Zora said, for she seemed to be constitutionally incapable of going along when it came to her mother's wishes. "It's a genuine gift."

"Folderol and gibbering," Mrs. Stewart replied.

Offended, Zora deliberately slung an arm. "You're wounding her."

"I'm fine," I said, swallowing a hiccupping laugh at the look she gave me. "Besides, I couldn't possibly take callers from Annapolis *and* Baltimore, so perhaps it's best to keep our diversions to ourselves."

"That's what I like to hear. It's a long week-end, Amelia — do your best to rub off on her." Mrs. Stewart made an expression very like a smirk, though she was entirely too well-bred to smirk on the street.

Zora rested her head against mine. "For that, I'm running away with an actor."

"Good luck finding an actor who could keep you in tea," Mrs. Stewart muttered. Satisfied that we would lose neither our bags nor our virtue on the road, she stepped down. A plume of dust rose at her hems, earth pounded tender by the constant fall of boots and horseshoes.

Heaving a sigh, Zora said, "I wish you'd take us."

"Five ladies alone on the road, I think not." Mrs. Stewart laughed incredulously. "Your father is a perfectly good driver."

"He's slow as sap," Zora confided.

Her breath tickled my ear, her voice buzzing in it, and that set me to laughing again. It matched the delicious buzz in my chest, the keen pitch of anticipation rising by the moment. Oh, how endless seemed the skies above Baltimore, how pure the clouds that rushed on their currents out to sea!

We had good weather ahead. And good company planned, because as soon as Zora's father found his way to the victoria, we'd collect Sarah and Mattie for our long week-end in Annapolis. For our first taste of freedom! For my second city dance!

For my chance to return Nathaniel's glove in person.

When Mr. Stewart finally appeared, Mrs. Stewart hurried to throw last-minute admonishments at us.

"See you're on your best behavior, and mind Mrs.

Castillo as if she were me." Thinking better of that advice, she interrupted herself. "As if she were anyone *but* me."

"Well, so much for arguing that exception," I told Zora, and we melted to giddy laughter once again.

※ ※ ※

In dumbfounded wonder, I stared at the mansion spread before us in Annapolis.

When we'd turned off the pressed dirt road onto a brick-paved way, I had thought perhaps that we might have come into the city by backward means. But the curve in the drive straightened, revealing Tammany House. It was a grand, sprawling palace to me.

The main house stood three stories, with tall windows evenly spaced across the façade. And should that have been its entirety, I would have marveled. But Tammany House continued, with wings spread out on either side. And there were balustraded patios, meant for lounging.

I only had to close my eyes to imagine standing up there to take in the stars. Or the sunset. Maybe this is where I would finally capture a glimpse of my own future.

"It's something, isn't it?" Sarah said, her eyes full of glory.

Her smile curled at one corner, somehow at once wistful and proud. She gazed on Tammany House as if it were a prize. Something to be won, but in what game of chance, I didn't know. It seemed unlikely that Mrs. Castillo would give her domain to a girl unrelated to her, and I understood that the family had a single daughter and no sons. Should Sarah aspire to have Tammany House for herself, she would have to take it by supernatural means, indeed.

It was grand, too grand to even realize, when Mr. Stewart took us inside. I lost myself in the introductions to Mrs. Castillo, so drunk was I on the details around me.

Art and sculpture, crystal and glass—raucous colors gave way to quiet ones as a maid led us up a spiraling staircase. The ceilings rose so high, embellished in every corner. Yet our footsteps hardly echoed for the luxuriously thick carpet that coursed the halls like a claret river.

"This is too much," I whispered to Zora, when the maid opened the door to our bedroom. I was almost sick with it, trying to grasp that I should be staying in this velvet room, sleeping in that curtained bed, breakfasting on that walk just outside the window.

Wryly, Zora pushed me into the room. "The Castillos have had some modest success in shipping."

"And they are your cousins?" I asked, suddenly laughing at myself for my timid meeting of this fine estate. As grand as it was, it was naught more than bricks and timbers. I should have found it no more frightening than a broomstick.

Skirting around me, Zora held her arms out and spun in the wide open of the chamber. In spite of the dust on her gown, with her bonnet still fixed, she stepped onto the trunk at the foot of the bed, then fell straight back into the mounds of pillows. "Mama's cousins, by marriage. Consequently, the Castillos are nothing at all to us, but generous because they can be."

"Zora!"

A sleek girl still in braids cut around me, as if I didn't exist at all. She filled up the room with a nasal twang. "Why aren't you changing? Mama likes to serve at seven. I already told Sarah."

Edging toward the window, I caught a glimpse of the horror smearing across Zora's delicate features. She seemed very much a caricature of herself as she struggled to sit up. "We'll see to it once our bags are delivered, Agnes."

Agnes rounded on me, squinting as she approached. She was a tiny general, her service to the cause measured in silk ribbons and bows. "Is that the best dress you have?"

"No," I said, trying not to bark with laughter. "I'll make myself presentable, I swear it."

She stood a moment more, as if she doubted that I could ever be made presentable, but then huffed her satisfaction. "All right, then. Seven o'clock, remember. Mama—"

"Serves precisely at seven," Zora muttered. "Yes, thank you."

As soon as Agnes marched away, I hurried to help Zora off her back. Instead, the awful wretch clasped my arms and dragged me into the quiet dark of the canopy with her. We'd have to roll off. What a charming display of our grace and civility that would be.

"We're a mess," I said, collapsing in soft giggles. The brocade above us swam with fishes and birds, and I couldn't help but chase them with my gaze.

"Did I say the Castillos kept us out of generosity alone?" Zora asked.

"You did."

With a great sigh, she covered her face and said, "Well, I lied. They keep us so Agnes might play at having friends."

❋ ❋ ❋

"We could be bothering them," Mattie whispered.

"We're *deliberately* bothering them," Sarah replied, throwing back the curtains round our bed.

Though we should have been sleeping, none of us could, and Zora and I scrambled around to make room for them. We looked like a tumult of wildflowers, all puffed up in our white lace sleeping gowns on the emerald field of our bedding.

Mattie curled at the foot. Want of slumber softened her already gentle features, and she stroked the bedcover as if it were a beloved kitten. "Can you hardly wait for tomorrow, Amelia?"

"I can't," I said. I curled my arms above my head, tugging at the plaits that would save me an hour's dressing with hot irons. "The first dance drove me to distraction. This one will set me on the road to madness and ruin."

"It's Mr. Witherspoon who does that," Zora teased.

But I refused to blush. "It was a wicked, wonderful thing, inviting me the way he did."

Sarah pressed her toe against Mattie's knee, harmlessly menacing her by rocking her back and forth. The bed quaked with the motion, like an ocean beneath us, the lazy sway of waves in the dark. "You can't marry him, you realize."

"He didn't ask," I replied smartly. Of one thing I was entirely certain: Nathaniel Witherspoon was not the marriageable material that my brother sent me to find. Actually, there was one more thing of certainty: at that moment, I didn't care.

Undeterred, Mattie nattered on.

"We won't find *anyone* to marry here. Mr. Witherspoon is unsuitable. We're all hopeless," Mattie said. She seemed untroubled by this, but then troubled, as she was quick to include, "Save you, Zora. Although you found Thomas in Baltimore. You're only reinforcing him here."

For once, Zora turned scarlet, so bright I was tempted to press my cold hand to her cheeks to warm them. "And yet neither has he asked, thank you."

"He only needs time." Sarah stretched once more, then spilled across the bed in a lazy puddle. "His father's apprenticing him. He won't need to go away to study, and fast as you know it, his name will be on the sign beside the door as well."

Frowning, I peered over at her. "You can't apprentice medicine. There are schools for it. Licenses to be had."

Zora settled with her hands folded on her chest. "Some of them are apprenticed, I think."

"Anyone may call himself a doctor," Mattie said. She wound a loose curl round and round her finger, and seemed to drift before remembering the rest of her thought. "And if there's no harm done—"

"The point," Sarah said, cutting Mattie off and recovering the conversation from its digression, "is that he'll be able to keep a wife soon, which means he'll want one."

"Does a man ever *want* one?" Zora asked.

"I should think Thomas does, and no doubt you're the one he'll ask for." At that, I pressed my hand to her cheek, smiling fondly.

"And you'll tell us every little thing." Sarah's declaration carried about it some certainty.

"What makes you think I'd speak secrets from our marriage bed?" Zora demanded, sitting up. "You do me a grave disservice, Sarah Holbrook!"

For a moment we all held silent, for Zora's ire sounded entirely too real. The crude intimation that there should be something to tell hung there, ripe and round, glaring so until Zora rolled her eyes and gave Sarah a shove. "Oh, if I had a glass, that you could see yourself right now!"

"Harpy," Sarah replied.

Collapsing, Zora declared, "Right now, all I want to be is the thing that distracts him and troubles him and sweetly disturbs him from morning 'til night."

"I should want to be a wife," Mattie said, sighing thoughtfully. "And a mother. I'm fond of babies."

Bemused, Sarah said, "I will marry, but only beneath me."

"You're so cruel, pretending Caleb has no intentions," Mattie said.

"Those are his intentions, not mine." Swimming in the sheets, Sarah turned and twisted, giving Mattie a little shove before settling again.

Mattie said, "I'd never marry down," but it came out a bit plaintive.

Dissolving against Sarah's shoulder, Zora told Mattie, "You may have to. We're hardly up!"

I giggled along—as if I hadn't set myself on the most unsuitable beau of all. Blinding myself willfully to it, I gave into merriment.

How we laughed, at that and a hundred other jests between midnight and morning—the glorious morning that would bring, at last, the dawning of my next waltz with Nathaniel.

Thirteen

I WAS SO EXCITED this morning," I told Zora as we wound our way through the refreshment room. "Why do I feel so ill now?"

Knowingly, Zora turned back to me, blocking the punch bowl for all comers, without the first indication that she cared. "It's anticipation. I told you to have that nerve tonic."

"It smelled like a . . . I can't even say it in polite company."

"Well, I had some and look at me." Zora slipped her arm into mine, leading me along again. "Fine and fit and barely ready to have hysterics, considering it seems we're here entirely alone."

And with that, she gave voice to my distress.

Walking through the arch of Sienna Place had been very much an entrance to a fantasy. Under Mrs. Castillo's thoughtful gaze, we fashionably arrived an hour after the start and paid our way with new quarters. In exchange, a boy in a Grecian costume and golden diadem, presumably Apollo himself, offered us dance cards.

Past him, in the ballroom itself, tempered jets glowed along the walls and in ornate sunburst chandeliers overhead. Organza bunting, shimmering like sunlight on a lake, draped the windows, some opened to let out the heat, some closed to keep out the night. Dancing here, conversing there—the ballroom gleamed with all the jewels of respectable society.

Mrs. Castillo excused herself to sit with the other married ladies, no doubt thinking the four of us should manage quite well to chaperone one another with only an occasional glimpse from her to measure our manners.

"We'll sit over there," Mattie told us, soon after Mrs. Castillo took her leave.

She nodded at seats empty by the far windows—seats rather near a clutch of young men gesturing among themselves. Sarah swept her fan open, gazing mysteriously over its lace trim. Though she played at flirtatiousness, her voice came laced with sarcasm.

"Wish us luck on our fishing expedition, ladies."

Amused, we watched them go. As Mattie intended to dance as many dances as she could and Sarah needed time to introduce herself to the carpenters and musicians, apparently, they were wise to separate from us. *We* avoided too-long looks and pretended hem distress, all to the goal of saving ourselves and our cards for two alone.

"I've only just realized," I said, trying to keep bitterness from creeping into my voice, "you're the one who has an actual beau."

"Is there something on your mind?"

We turned our third circuit past the refreshment table, and I stopped to have some punch. I wondered what had turned it such a cloudy shade of storm, and when I took a sip, I had my answer. Lime, tart, teasing lime that left me puckering. "It's just . . . it only just occurred to me that your invitation was made in the plain, but mine came by treachery."

Zora coughed on her punch and looked askance at me. "By treachery? Have we found ourselves at a pirates' ball?"

"Mock if you will, but it's true. If Mr. Witherspoon finds himself otherwise diverted tonight, then I'm his fool. There's nothing I can do about it. We're the only ones who know he was obligated to me at all."

Tipping her cup, Zora seemed to dare herself to take another startling sip. "He went to such trouble to lure you. What could he possibly gain by playing you false?"

Nothing, I started to say, but the word refused to come. For he delighted, again and again, in unsettling me—would this not be the greatest unsettlement of them all? Reason told me that Thomas would suffer before making himself a party to such a plot. But logic told me that if Nathaniel wanted to lie to me, he could lie to Thomas just as easily.

"Stop it," Zora scolded.

"I didn't speak!"

"Your pinched little face did." Zora abandoned her punch. "You're lovely tonight, and he would be the lowest sort to summon you without intent."

Carrying my cup along, I followed Zora in her nervous promenade around the room once more. "He'd have no way of knowing how lovely I am if he doesn't appear."

Zora shook her fan at me. "Away. Out of my sight, you moping chit."

With a grumble, I stepped to let her pass, then fell in behind her to make our way toward the ballroom. I thought about stepping on the lace train of her Watteau, although that wouldn't really please me. It would just annoy her. Two foul tempers at a dance instead of one—that wouldn't improve anything.

"Thomas," Zora breathed.

She stopped so abruptly that I splashed my ridiculously bare chest with punch. Due to the bend of my gown's basque, the spill drained into my corset. It was half a blessing. My gown showed no evidence of a stain, but I felt it growing sticky and warm against my skin.

"Is Mr. Witherspoon with him?" I searched my clutch for a kerchief and said, before she had the chance to reply, "I take that to mean no."

"You've no need to be cross with me." Zora took my hand, pulling me along to put herself in Thomas' gaze.

Still daubing myself dry, I said, "I'm only asking."

With impeccable manners, Thomas made his way around the floor, an interminable progress to watch with Zora all but jittering beside me. The fine union blue of his coat suited him.

"How much could he possibly say to Mattie?" Zora asked, impatient.

I didn't answer. They should have been together, Thomas and Nathaniel. They should have been early to greet us. What if our dance cards had filled early? Didn't they risk missing our charms completely by coming so late?

My throat tightened, and I hated the new sting of tears in my eyes. What an awful, spoiled thing I'd become to expect and to demand, when I should have counted myself lucky to spend even a single day outside my little village in Maine.

"Miss Stewart," Thomas said, once he finally reached our side of the ballroom. "Miss van den Broek."

I offered a game smile and silence in response. Fear clutched me, the certainty that if I tried to speak, I would only cry instead.

"Did you come alone?" Zora asked, the question half-sharpened and plaintive.

"Caleb's here with me to surprise Miss Holbrook, and . . ." When he realized what she really asked, he turned toward me, apologetic. "Mr. Witherspoon didn't drive in with us; I thought he'd be along on his own."

Clasping my throat, I tried to rub away the knot that had formed there. Now managing to speak, I sounded stilted and formal. Well, if nothing else, I had my manners. "I thank you most kindly, Mr. Rea."

Thomas held out a gallant hand. "Shall I have the honor of dancing this set with you, Miss van den Broek?"

"May I write you in for the schottische after the interval? I haven't looked in on Mrs. Castillo in an hour, and truly I should."

"I would be honored," Thomas said, and if he was relieved to escape me, he showed it not at all. *For Thomas,* I told myself, as I fled to take some air and another dip of awful punch, *was a gentleman.*

And *I* was a fool.

☀ ☀ ☀

I suppose I should have, when splitting myself off from my chaperones, slipped into the garden. The illicit thrill of going about in the dark might have cheered me. Instead, I submitted to the melancholy of exploring this grand hall alone.

Taking the stairs, I found the ladies' salon, where summer blooms in all shades sat, resting, fanning the sweat from their faces and mending their gowns. A kind, round woman turned to me. Her smile said that I could come inside if I wished.

I nodded my thanks and moved on.

The music downstairs became a whisper as I retreated down the hall. The gaslights dimmed gradually, until I found myself at a bend where none glowed at all. For a moment, I thought I might go back, but why?

All I had was an empty dance card and the awful realization that I had been rash. I'd been a fool. I'd let Nathaniel insinuate himself into my life. For nothing—for a kiss on the wrist and a dark, teasing look.

How stupid I was.

My inclination the first night, when I denied him on account of all my possibilities for the summer—that was the right one. I had no business playing at intrigue; I'd failed entirely at my single task for the summer by setting my heart on a painter, a Fourteenth—a rogue. If I'd had the slightest sense, I should have returned to the ball and filled my card. I should have stolen Sarah's fan tricks and started my summer work in truth.

But I didn't.

I lifted my skirts and ventured on. The distant cry of violins urged, the delectable cool of shadows tempted. I gave in, slipping into a dreamy haze of wonder at fine things I could never hope to own and elegant solitudes I could enjoy but this once.

A door drifted open at the end of the hall. At first, I hesitated, for what if I should stumble on things never meant for my eyes? But then my boldness reasserted itself—before me now were shadowed busts and paintings. A few more steps indicted me no more than the hundred I'd already taken.

Daring swept over me as I brushed the door open. No conspirators looked up from a map; no lovers gasped, caught by my unexpected appearance. It was just a room, tastefully appointed, but with nothing to recommend it over any other. Fine curtains parted at the window, drifting on a breeze.

Before me, a lawn traced in bluesilver shadow spread into the night. The moon hung low. It glittered like a curved needle, left in a field of midnight velvet.

Clasping the balcony rail, I lifted my face to the wind again. It carried the cold, stony scent of fresh water. All my life, the ocean had surrounded me, saltily pushing me to the west.

This spring's sweetness offered to carry me away, off to cold, clear lands that I had yet begun to imagine. Eyes closed, I pressed forward a bit more, parting my lips to catch a taste of that promise.

"Don't jump," Nathaniel murmured beside me.

Though my breath faltered, I could, at last, face him. Seeing him thrilled me as ever. I was helplessly attracted to his wanton mouth. But now I looked on him without illusion. Whatever method he took to slip in and out unannounced, it no longer impressed me.

"Over you? I should hardly think so."

"You're angry," he said. And as if nothing had passed between us but days since our last meeting, he let his black gaze trace the path of my lips. "I'm unforgivably late. Can we come to an accord, Miss van den Broek?"

"I don't practice diplomacy, and you seem incapable of it," I said. I felt as though something wound in me, tighter and tighter, threatening to snap. Fumbling with the clasp on my bag, I finally mastered it and pulled out his glove.

"Please don't," he said. His expression offered the first tantalizing glimpse of vulnerability—the faintest furrow of his brow.

In that moment, I thought to smooth it away. And in that moment, I chose not to because everything I'd said to Zora was still true. He called on me in secret, and no good could come of meeting him secretly.

"I permitted too many liberties. You lacked the grace to refuse them."

Nathaniel took my hand rather than his glove and filled the space between us. A struggle played out on his face, tugging brow and mouth in disparate directions. Finally, as if pained when the words tore from his lips, he said, "I couldn't afford my share of the cab."

"How can that be?" I asked, ignoring the way spring came to my blood, melting my icy resolve in an instant. But I hid it. The wisest thing for both of us would be to close this play. "Aren't you a man of independent means? Don't you do as you please?"

"I paint portraits to pay my rent," he said, his nostrils

flaring. Oh, his confidence and pride, how strange to see them shaken. "I take dinners with the vain and superstitious to buy my canvas and oils."

Softening the slightest, I cast my gaze from his light and murmured, "Mr. Witherspoon . . ."

"So, if by saying I scrabble to have what I have and claw to keep it, then I suppose I do very much do as I please. I beg you look at me." And though he could have, though I'd seen it happen to other girls, Nathaniel didn't shake me. And he didn't force my eyes to meet his. He simply said once more, "I beg you."

"How do you come and go?" I asked. Though I peered yet at the sky, a warm, ornate pattern traced my skin, the traverse of his gaze. "I want a secret of yours. Answer me that."

"In mist," he said, but it was with laughter. "In shadows. As a hawk? What would you have me tell you?"

At that I turned, stumbling into the dark briars of his eyes meeting mine. "The truth."

"I go on foot, as any man." He didn't waver, but he did squeeze my hand and murmur, "And sometimes I send myself to you in the wind, for you come to me in my thoughts."

Starting to shiver, I shook my head. "I haven't. I wouldn't know how."

He raised his hand, a length of black ribbon wrapped around it. A charm dangled from it, an amber sun in silver, radiating with waves of light that came to points. Didn't I know then? On the last rays of daylight, opened to that place where our spirits moved freely when our bodies did not—his charm was my answer.

Without thinking, I touched my throat and turned, but not to leave him. He unfurled the length of ribbon and framed my body between his arms as I leaned back to his chest—the steps of this dance inspired by some outward force.

Slipping the choker round my neck, he took care to fasten it, touching skin and charm to place it perfectly. Then he caught my eye in the window's glass, and how handsome a pair were we.

"You speak into me," he whispered, just behind my ear. "So I come."

My throat went dry. Touching the warming pendant, I looked back, though not directly at him. "Mr. Witherspoon—"

Cutting me off again, he said, "You speak into me, Amelia."

"And so you come . . ." I parted my lips to offer his name, but he stole my kiss instead.

Fourteen

I N THE DARK RECESSES of our bed at Tammany House, I
still felt the burn of dancing in my limbs.

My legs skimmed restlessly between the sheets. Strok-
ing the length of velvet around my throat was like running
my fingers through a hot bath. It held a secret—if I rubbed
against the grain, a hint of Nathaniel's bay rum rose up to
spark my heart.

Turning, twisting toward a waltz, I must have sighed
aloud, for Zora sat up and slapped the sheets between us.

"Would you lie still?"

"I'm hardly moving," I replied, tugging her back down.
"Come talk to me."

Zora rose once more, taking her pillow to punch back into shape. "It's late, Amelia. I'm tired."

"You're in one of your moods," I said—petulantly, I admit. When Nathaniel and I rejoined the ball, her smile never faltered, but a distinct chill inhabited it. That frost hung between us yet, and I didn't care for it.

"It's nearly morning," she replied, tossing her pillow carelessly in place, to fall upon it. She faced me in the dark, brave enough at least to present her cold front directly.

"Thomas was late, too," I said. I pulled the blankets to my chin, my restlessness turned nervousness with confrontation. "Nathaniel explained himself. He apologized."

Ignoring that, Zora said, "You wrote Thomas in for the schottische and never appeared for it."

"You should have danced it with him!" It was my turn to sit up, for arguing in recline only made my stomach churn.

"He asked you!"

"For your sake, not mine!"

As there were truths in all the things we said, we fell silent. Wrapping my arms around myself, I fixed my gaze on the brocade curtains.

Fish leaped, again and again, an endless pattern that ceased only at the sewn edge of their ocean. I didn't want to stay at odds with Zora. And she didn't either—we proved our affection when we spoke at the same time.

"No, you," I murmured, daring to look in her direction.

"I don't want to give Mama a victory," Zora said. She clasped her toes through the covers and sighed. "But she could have been right, you know. About keeping us from boys who ignore all rules of courtship."

Stung, I drew back. "What an easy conclusion to make when your sweetheart *can* court you."

"Would you want yours to?"

"Of course," I said, but I wondered at myself. I wondered if I lied.

Once, I had compared Thomas' sweetness to Nathaniel's shamelessness and found the former entirely lacking. No fire burned hot without constant stirring. How ordinary a banked flame could seem. Even the tragedy of realizing I could have been Nathaniel's fool—but wasn't—made his lips on mine that much more intoxicating. Every time I worried about wanting to be a proper lady, he came along to remind me that I didn't care for duty and goodness.

Tenderly, Zora touched my brow and my cheek. "You know it's not disapproval. I like him well enough."

I twisted myself around, curling up and laying my head on her lap. "He says I speak into him."

"Well, he *should* say pretty things," Zora replied.

"It's more than that," I said. "I call out, and he appears. Like I'm the only firefly in the dark for him."

Zora smoothed my hair. Her touch was so gentle, I might not have realized it, if the scent of her rose water hadn't washed away Nathaniel's bay rum. "Well, I have a solution, I suppose."

I asked, "Have you?"

"Look into the sunset, and see if the answer is writ there."

How simple an answer, and yet one that now terrified me. What if I should see him cloaked for his wedding day to some other? What if I should see him broken and dying?

And yet the molten gold of Sarah's fate had not been set because I saw it. Hardly so! She would have been so much worse off if I'd never looked. So many thoughts swirled around me, I found it hard to settle on just one. I turned to confidences instead.

"Before we danced, he met me alone on the balcony."

"Amelia!" Zora blinked at me, equal parts scandalized and delighted. She answered in a whisper of her own, as if wicked secrets carried more readily than ordinary conversation. "What happened?"

I pressed my fingers to the setting sun at my throat, quiet for a long moment. Then, at last, I said, "Everything."

❊ ❊ ❊

"Chase me," Agnes shouted at a fat little puppy who wanted nothing but a nap in Mattie's skirts.

We had spread out on the lawn to enjoy a late picnic, and it was pleasant enough except for Agnes' constant interruptions. Mattie coddled her the best, but even *she* resorted to chattering about her geometry lessons. Agnes couldn't abide figures, so that ran her off neatly—for a while.

"Come on, Sullivan!" Rounding back toward our blanket, Agnes whistled and clapped her hands. "Come on!"

Under her breath, Sarah urged Mattie, "For all that's holy, give him up. *Please.*"

Mattie sighed, then set the white puffed pup on his feet. With a firm nudge, she sent him staggering onto the lawn, where Agnes finally caught his attention with a little stick.

"He was perfectly happy," Mattie said.

Sarah shrugged, not at all apologetic. "He was the only one."

Laughing, I wished I could lounge back on my elbows

like the boys did. Perhaps, for that moment, I wished I could kick off my shoes and play barefoot on the grass and fly along the brook in the distance without a care. If there were some way to do all of that and keep my new walking dress, too, I should have been blessed, indeed.

Fortunately, the violet embroidered checks on my polonaise so delighted me that I could satisfy myself by running bare fingers across them. It was rather like strumming a tiny picket fence, a childish amusement, perhaps. But amuse me, it did.

"Where have you got to?" Sarah asked, leaning across our empty basket to wave fingers in my face.

"Oh, she's in love," Zora said. "Haven't you heard?"

Sarah stopped picking at her lemon cake. "Are you? With Mr. Witherspoon?"

"Rich man, poor man, whom shall I wed?" Mattie sang, clasping her hands together and turning her face to the sky—play-acting at my expense.

"You think overmuch about proposals," I said.

"Isn't that where it all leads?"

Zora groaned. "Surrender! We surrender! You marriage-sick wretch! Let us have our romances first!"

"I shall get married one day," Agnes announced, pressing her hands to her chest. "My husband will be a sea captain.

And he will sail to extraordinary places! And return to me with untold riches."

"There you go," I told Mattie, and didn't even try to hide my laughter. "You've found your kindred in Agnes."

Taking that for an invitation, Agnes abandoned Sullivan and threw herself onto the blanket. Still too young for a corset, she had the freedom to wallow in the tightest of spaces, and, to our delight, the space she chose was the crook of Sarah's arm. "Who will you marry?"

Sarah glowered at us but answered once more, "Someone who works for a living."

"Oh." Agnes had not the guile developed to hide her disdain. "Well, I won't."

"A sea captain," Mattie repeated, daring to goad Sarah with a most innocent expression. Pride swelled in my breast for her, for taking the shot when it presented itself. I wondered if I worried overmuch about Mattie's ability to fend for herself.

Agnes fingered the lace hem of her skirt, thoughtful. "And we will have nothing but sons. Four of them. I've dreamed it, you know."

"A premonition in a dream, really?" Sarah drawled — and, oh, at once, I saw the retribution in her eyes. She slipped an arm around Agnes' shoulder and pointed to me. "Amelia can see the future."

I waved at the suggestion. "Only at twilight. And only for grown ladies, I'm afraid."

"You're not grown," Agnes pointed out. How I loathed the crow-like rasping of her voice.

"In any case, you've dreamed your future," I said. "I'm sure my sendings would agree. Sea captain for a husband, four handsome sons."

"They're not handsome," Agnes said. She corrected me as she stood. "They're babies."

Reclaiming Sullivan when he nosed in for a taste of cake, Mattie wrapped her arms around the puppy and smiled at Agnes. "Babies do grow up."

"Mine don't," Agnes told her. "They all die."

With that, she skipped off across the lawn. Throwing her arms out, she seemed to embrace the sky, spinning and tumbling across it like the puff of a dandelion set free. We watched her in quiet for a moment, suspended by her terrible dream. Zora broke first.

"That child is strange," she said, gathering dishes to take inside.

"You should look," Mattie told me.

I cast a wary glance to the west. The blue sky had darkened with clouds, waiting to swallow the sun. I wondered if I really did need the light to see. Then I shuddered to think of seeking out something so awful as Agnes' dream babies.

"I don't want to, Mattie. I don't just see; I live it. Like I'm in the moment."

"Ohhh," she breathed. Then, rubbing her cheek against the pup's, she asked, "What would happen if you foretold someone's death, I wonder?"

I chilled. "I wouldn't know."

As if this had all been a mental exercise, like a game of I Spy gone philosophical, Mattie offered a smile and a new subject to discuss. "Do you think we'll have had many callers in our absence?"

"We can hope," I said, forcing false cheer. "And hope alone. Some things are better left to the mysteries of time."

❋ ❋ ❋

The glory of Baltimore had dimmed not at all during our time in Annapolis. It seemed more real to me, more honest with its brick-faced row houses standing as soldiers and its parlors tight and cozy.

Good, sweet scents greeted us when we came through the door. Good, sweet Mrs. Stewart, softened by our days away, greeted us with cinnamon-dusted embraces.

"Back here," she said, hustling us toward the kitchen. "Let's hear all of it."

"We behaved," Zora said, dropping into a chair by the back door.

Holding a bowl of brandied raisins out, Mrs. Stewart waited for me to take one, then offered the bowl to Zora. "I know that; you're good girls. Did you fill your dance cards?"

"Nearly," I said, rolling the plump fruit between my fingers. "My corset's stained with punch."

Zora nodded. "It is. We rubbed it with vinegar, and now it smells like pickled limes."

Mrs. Stewart busied herself at the oven, leaning over to peer at her bread. "I don't think your brother sent enough for a new corset, Amelia, but we can see."

"Since I'm the only one sniffing it, I imagine I'll survive the insult," I said.

"Thrift," Mrs. Stewart said, letting the iron door clang closed again. "It's a good quality to have."

"What's all this for?" Zora asked, reaching for another raisin and nodding toward the extensive spread of sweets and breads that covered the counters. "Are you having a party?"

Mrs. Stewart straightened up, smoothing her hair from her sweat-damp brow. "As if I could afford you and a party besides. No, these are to take on your calls."

"What calls?"

Plucking a familiar box from the shelf, Mrs. Stewart turned its contents out on the table. A rain of cards spilled out, fifty at least!

Immediately on our feet, Zora and I pressed against the table, reaching into the bounty. Choosing randomly, we both pulled out cards *pour présenter*. Name after name, few familiar, all clamoring for our company.

It had been steady before our trip, but this! It seemed like an entire phalanx—all hoping I could be their conduit to the sunset beyond.

And against all reason, I could hardly wait.

Barely home, and we went off again, Zora and I. I had tucked in my bag an entire clasp of my new calling cards, finally lifted from their boxes and granted, as tickets, to the front doors of what seemed like every row house in Reservoir Hill.

Though crowding crushes continually left me overexerted, I began to appreciate the joys of a wide circle met in small increments.

Some plied us with sweets, and others with clean copies of their cards, for it seemed lately that it was fashionable to make collections of them. "Do come back," they all said, leaning out their doors to judge the sky. Calling hours could last only so long, and I apologized again and again that I had but the briefest window into the future.

And trust Zora to make the most of that window, indeed. She'd spent the morning arranging us, deciding who might wait, and whom we wouldn't care to see at all, but of greatest importance would be those who took our visit closest to dusk.

This is how we came to present ourselves at Caleb Grey's door just as the shadows grew long. It was a curiosity, for the card in our box had actually been marked Lucy Grey—Caleb's baby sister, who couldn't have possibly invited us on her own. We weren't meant to call on young men unless we had business with them, so it was a clever lure, we both agreed.

"Hurry," he said, peering around us to see who might glimpse us at his door, and then closing it quickly to silence any possible rumors.

We followed him not to the parlor but to a music room —
small but handsomely appointed, with a pianoforte at the
window and violins sitting in their hooks on the shelf.

Absurdly, I longed to pluck the strings, just to hear them
hum, a remnant of the ball recaptured and released.

"I'm sorry to compromise you," Caleb said, his face
drawn.

For he had, in truth, done just that. Caleb was no cousin
to Zora, and no friend even to me. Though Zora and I chap-
eroned each other, there would be no end to the stain on our
reputations if it was known that we met alone with boys in
their houses. We were naughty enough to take correspon-
dence and steal kisses in the ballroom's shadows.

But Zora knew him well. Quiet with concern and uncon-
cerned with propriety, she caught his chin in her hand and
raised his face to meet hers. "What's the matter, then?"

Turning to me, Caleb came too close, then jumped back
a step, as if caught by a spark. Something dark moved
through his expression, a wildness — a terror that I couldn't
quite name. How many times had Nathaniel thrilled me
with his inconstancy? But Caleb's same temperament frightened me.

"How do you see?" he demanded.

I stammered, "Is there some question I could . . ."

Caleb pressed closer, but Zora stayed him. "If you can't reveal your distress, how can she possibly illuminate it?"

Fire seemed to travel beneath his skin, leaping from place to place, and giving, altogether, an impression of a blaze far greater than his body could contain. Finally, his voice rough and defeated, he said, "Sarah. That's my distress. Ask for nothing more, I beg you."

"That's not a question," I said.

Another flare of temper blackened his eyes. "Mind your place and ask for nothing more!"

"Mind your manners," Zora snapped.

He tried to brush her aside, reaching once more for me — as if he had some right to put his hands on my personage, after luring me to his house by trickery. "You read for anyone, why not me?"

Zora intervened. To be specific, she rapped him on the arm with her bag. Quite honestly, if she'd had a newspaper, I think she would have rolled and wielded it, as if he were a misbehaving puppy.

Then she offered me her elbow and said, "We'll be going. We've got hundreds of callers who won't abuse the mystic."

Lunging in front of us, Caleb all but threw himself against

the door. I really thought he might try to lock us in. Struggling from the inside out, his mouth twisted uncomfortably, until it finally settled into something like a smile. Slowly, he said to me in a forced voice, "I apologize, Miss van den Broek. Please stay."

Zora shook her head slightly, but I wavered. Shamefully, I longed to know more—for my first impression of Sarah and Caleb was of two magnets, held apart only by force. But everything Sarah had said since, that she cared not for Caleb's intentions and intended to marry beneath her—I admit it, I hungered for a taste of gossip.

"Very well," I said, swallowing down nervousness. We returned to the music room, sunlight making threats on the strings of the violins. I took a chair that turned my gaze to the window and offered a hand. "Think on her, and I shall try."

Caleb grasped my hand, rather too hard, but I bore it with grace. His skin felt so hot as to be fevered. Beneath his skin, he quavered, a tight trembling that disconcerted me entirely. Thus, with trepidation I took my clearing breaths, spilling myself out so the sunset might pour in.

A crimson beam streaked across my face, a rosy sunset full of wine hues, extraordinary to admire but different from the usual gold that tempted my sight.

I drew again, exhaled once more, gazing with a blinkless stare that took in no more and no less than the window and the aventurine curtains that surrounded it.

Just when I lifted my face to offer my condolences, the world turned scarlet. Not an intimation of it—all was scarlet, in truth.

Warily, I moved, for I felt very much myself *inside* this sending, as if I could stand up and wander the Greys' house unseen. As if I had only taken a step to the side, instead of a leap toward the future.

The weight of a gaze touched my bare neck; I felt the hair rise. I said, *Nathaniel.*

And he answered, *Are you well?*

Coming round to face him, I circled and circled, examining the shape of him in this vision, the shade of him. *Are you yourself? Or is this only sight?*

Both?

We had an awareness here, a privilege of motion I hadn't felt before when calling on the vespers. *I* took this moment; it didn't take me.

Part of me very much wondered what Caleb and Zora saw as I approached Nathaniel; did I sit still in my chair, frozen? Did I fall and fit before them, in Privalovna's hysterical way?

I'm looking for Sarah, I said, but as the words slipped out, they lost meaning for me.

I wanted to press myself into Nathaniel's arms; I wondered if here, he could loop his fingers in my hair and kiss me again with no fear of reprisal. I didn't know what my flesh might do, so I held back. My lips stung in memory, in desire. A look, I decided—I could satisfy myself with a look.

Nathaniel felt no such hesitation. His hands bare, he dared frame my face with them. His thumbs swept at once, beneath my lip and up to trace the curve of my cheeks. *I would say, then, you haven't found her.*

"Nathaniel." My lashes sank, gentle in spite of the painful winding of anticipation that gripped me otherwise.

"Amelia," he answered, but suddenly his voice was not his voice.

Snapping my eyes open, I peered up into Caleb Grey's face. Oh, I could have wept, distraught with frustration, but likewise relief that I came to in my chair. My trance had, if nothing else, turned Caleb pale and still, water on the fire that devoured him from within.

"I see nothing," I told him.

He shook as he blew out a breath. "And that means?"

To comfort, I offered a smile. "I've seen tragedy before.

Whatever mysteries you have remain, Caleb, but . . . if you tremble, I would fear not."

How I believed that as I spoke it; how very boastful my certainty sounded. Oh, the pride.

My terrible, terrible pride.

Fifteen

I T SEEMED OF LATE, I sat nothing but sunsets. The whirl-wind of it scarcely taxed me, but soon the clamor grew in a way that had the force of a demand behind it.

With the end of day so short, when a storm interfered with the light, I could only slip into so many visions. My path to the future was limited — at least, until the discovery on Camden Street.

I suppose I had never been entirely explicit about taking single callers, after speaking to Miss Lawrence, because I found myself in the middle of eight girls in an unfamiliar parlor. I recognized their sharp, hungry looks, though. They yearned for a vision, and this hostess, Miss Brosmer, pressed paper and pencil into my hand.

"I don't understand," I said, tipping my head back to gaze at her. "Didn't you wish me to see?"

Dropping herself into the chair beside me, she straightened a stack of papers, flattening them on top of a book before offering it all to me. "Have you heard of automatic writing? Mayhaps you could take down messages for all of us."

"She's never done it that way," Zora said. She came with me always, protecting and prodding me at turns, and I wouldn't have trusted myself to see without her.

"Couldn't you try?" Cutting her gaze toward the window, our hostess forced a pleasant smile.

I held the pencil with an uncertain grip. "I don't know . . ."

The brittle smile cracked, and Miss Brosmer asked quite bluntly, "Are you after a fee? We heard you don't take one."

Once when I'd been asked that, I trembled—now I burned. Did I have no good reputation? Did I not bring forth visions on command and give my gifts freely? It was an insult, and I put the pencil down sharply. "I most certainly do not, and you offend me greatly in the asking!"

"Then what's the matter?" she asked, though a worried murmur filled the room. I could see their eyes shifting, looking to me, then looking to the door. I could feel them vibrate with disappointment, to think I might leave them fortuneless.

Impressed with the weight and power of my rebuke, I reminded myself to be gracious still. Perhaps Zora called me Maine's Own Mystic, but I knew that I was yet a young woman who couldn't begin to explain how the sight came on her. Clearing my throat, I said gently, "You're just asking something of me that I've never done."

My retreat emboldened her. "Would it hurt to try? We read about it in *The Strand*," she said. It was a magazine full of fantastic stories, and I'd read it, too. Mediums opened themselves to the spirit world and let phantoms write with their hands.

I had no spirits. I had no guides. I had only the sunset. Fighting a sense of panic, I looked at the girls all around the table and shook. Raw with want, with need, they all watched me as if I alone could spare the meal to save them. What flare of pride and power I'd felt a moment before had fled me. It was cruel that my confidence never lingered.

With a look to Zora, I clutched the pencil once more and said, "All right. I can try."

Guessing at this, I started my breathing, then stopped. "Give me something. Anything, all of you, you'll have it back when I've finished. A glove."

"Hurry," Zora urged them. "The light's fading!"

The tea guests exchanged looks, but each stripped themselves of a glove. They piled up in my lap, lace and kid and satin, all in tasteful shades of cream or buff. I pushed my hand into the pile, balancing the paper and book on my knees. I felt awkward, but the worst of it, I felt inspected. Turning my eyes to the dimming light outside, I put the pencil to paper and waited.

Nothing came, and I blinked, shaking my head as I looked around to faces strangely drawn. "I'm sorry."

Zora wrapped a tight hand around my arm, so hard that my fingers flexed and the pencil flew from them. Before I could demand some explanation for her roughness, Miss Brosmer snatched the slips of paper from me, turning to pass them around.

"'Today in the vespers, I see the girl with the butterfly brooch at the druggist,'" read a red-haired girl, who wore, in fact, a butterfly brooch at her collar.

The lady beside her leaned over her shoulder to read, "'Today in the vespers, I hear a voice sweet as a nightingale gone hoarse just before a party.'"

A chill swept me, and I turned to Zora as another guest read, "'Today in the vespers, I see this day the same as the next, the same prospects held now to be the same prospects found three years hence.'"

That one burst into tears, and I murmured to Zora, "Did I write that?"

"And more," she said.

Miss Brosmer cleared her throat, lifting a paper before her face and reading, "'In the vespers, I see this lovely glove of crêpe and kid, gone missing and ruining the set.'" She lowered the page and squinted at me. "You've had us all on."

"I never claimed my visions were of consequence," I said stiffly. Taking to my feet, I shook the gloves from my skirt and returned both pencil and book to their perturbed owner.

Some complaints rose, but a fair girl at the end of the table snatched the paper from her neighbor's hand and fled to the kitchen. Her friends followed, a great clamor and demand for her to tell them the matter, and I thought it best that we go before they all turned on us.

Just as we made it to the door, Miss Brosmer came down the hall. "Wait!"

"Blasted latch," Zora cursed, rattling the doorknob, and then, when we found our egress too slow, turned to face whatever awful recrimination we had to bear to take our leave.

"I did apologize," I said weakly.

Waving a sheet of my predictions, she closed on us, less reading than repeating. "'Today in the vespers, I know that I am happy now he is dead.'"

"Oh, Amelia, you didn't," Zora said, a horrified whisper only for me, drowned out when our hostess spoke over her.

"I tell you in confidence that he's vicious. And I'm happy knowing she'll survive him."

Briskly, she pushed us out of the way, working the door's complicated latch to let us out. And then, as if this had been no more than an ordinary tea, she smiled first at Zora, then at me.

"May I have a card for my collection?" she asked.

Marveling at her quick shift, from skeptic to believer to . . . whatever this could be called, I gladly gave over my card just to pay my way from her foyer.

Zora fished one of hers from her clutch, and we thought ourselves on our way once we passed the threshold.

"How strange," Miss Brosmer said.

Poisonous curiosity drove me to turn back. "Is it?"

She held it up, rubbing the imprint of my name with her thumb. "The ink looks like blood."

And truth, in the slanting vermilion light, it did.

❊ ❊ ❊

"I'm not ready to go home," Zora said, hooking my arm with hers and pulling me toward Division Street once more.

Night came around us in a cooling cloak, a mantle happily taken after the heat of the day and the unfamiliar parlor.

"You mean, you've become accustomed to peeping at Thomas after a call and won't go home without it."

I teased, but I could hardly blame her. We passed Thomas Rea's yard nearly every day; we had reason to coincidentally find ourselves at his back fence.

But Mount Vernon Place, where the Fourteenths lived, remained a mystery to me. Bound by a tightness in my chest, I squeezed Zora's wrist and pulled her to stop with me.

"If you had business with Dr. Rea," I said, overtaken by an impetuous flash of heat. "Thomas could walk you home, could he not?"

"What business have I got with—" Zora stopped, eyes going round. "What sort of wickedness are you devising?"

"None," I swore. "And if I say nothing, you won't be implicated if I suffer some blow to my reputation."

"Amelia, can't we be clever about this?"

"In what way?" I turned myself out of her grasp, almost like the steps of a dance right on the sidewalk. "Invite only thirteen to a dinner party and hope upon hope that your father will hire him by chance? Send a letter begging him to call?"

Suddenly, near dark gave way to the oily glow of gaslight,

and night transformed. It seemed ragged around the edges, rougher and meaner than the city in the day. It frightened me; it delighted me.

"We can promenade the park tomorrow. Thomas would carry a note to him."

"And let's do that." I pressed fingers to my lips and stood by as a policeman came round the corner on his beat. Perfecting ourselves, Zora and I pretended to check our clutches at the good doctor's door, nodding pleasant greetings at the patrolman as he passed.

As soon as he went by, I whispered in Zora's ear. "Think of all the things you know that I couldn't possibly guess. How fine Thomas looks making firewood. How nicely he carries your parcels; how kindly he shares his last sharpened pencil. I have nothing like that, not one incidental memory to call my own."

"It's dangerous to go at night," Zora said.

Gently, I unwound myself from her grasp. "I'm sick with it, Zora."

No doubt, her thoughts spun, for she grasped at another excuse to keep me. "Do you even have his address? It's the whole heart of the city, Amelia, hardly a singular building unto itself."

"I don't need it," I said, then reached past her to rap on

Dr. Rea's door. The abruptness startled her. I held her pinned like a butterfly to a board.

Just as the door handle turned, Zora broke. "You must be back before eight o'clock."

I pressed a kiss and a promise to her cheek. "I'll say I went after a pomander for my corset. Thank you. Thank you a hundred times."

"I already regret this," she called after me, then clamped her mouth shut as the door swung open. "Dr. Rea, I apologize for the hour, but my throat's gone sore and Mama doesn't quite trust the new druggist at Eame's . . ."

✻ ✻ ✻

As I stepped from the cab, my driver frowned when I drew his wage from my purse. Instead of opening his hand to take my nickels, he leaned over the seat to ask, "What business do you have walking the park at this hour alone, miss?"

"Oh, I'm not alone," I told him, brazen as I could be. Casting my gaze out, I pointed at a pair of ladies in the distance. "See, there?"

Squinting, he took my coins but made no move to leave. "I'll sit and watch you meet them."

"You're a true gentleman, sir, thank you."

Steeling myself with a breath, I squared my shoulders and marched resolutely to those strange women, entirely unknown to me.

"Excuse me," I said.

Fortune had played me well, in choosing my imaginary companions. Their skirts swung like great black bells as they met me. "Yes, miss?"

I turned, waving the driver off. "I hate to trouble you, but do you have the time, perhaps?"

"Yes, of course. Ten past," one answered.

Warmly, I thanked her, my hands clasped in gratitude. When they walked on, so did I. My blood roared with satisfaction as I swept through the park.

Row houses lined a gentle slope, and I stared at them, one by one. This one had a red door, that one, blue. I considered them all, then stepped up to knock on the green one. It was the same shade as Nathaniel's stationery. I felt certain it would be right.

My certainty died when the door opened. Tall and bronze, a handsome young man considered me in curiosity. "May I help you?"

"I'm sorry to disturb you," I said, clutching my pendant. "I thought I might find Nathaniel Witherspoon here."

At once, he relaxed and turned to call out. "Nate! Company!"

I didn't have a chance to thank him before he walked away. I wasn't sure I wouldn't have laughed and danced and acted a fool in front of him, anyway. On magic alone, I'd found the right door.

And, oh, how the strength melted from me when Nathaniel came down the hall. He came in shirtsleeves, the linen stained with a wild play of color. For a moment, I closed my eyes, and when I opened them again, he stood before me, barefooted. He was mussed, bohemian and wild and . . . beautiful.

"Amelia," he said, pulling me inside.

For once, for the first time, he sounded urgent. Concerned. As if he might care about my reputation after all. The very idea amused me.

Clasping my hands together, I stood my straightest, as if I were a princess to be obeyed. "I'd like to see your studio, Mr. Witherspoon."

Nathaniel stepped into a loose pair of boots. "You shouldn't be in here. I can't believe Navid opened the door for you."

"How rude if he hadn't."

When Nathaniel turned to grab a jacket, I brushed past him. The acrid scent of turpentine burned my nose, and I followed it straight back. The scent deepened, with strange oils and perfumes. My heart raced, thrilled to be so surrounded by Nathaniel—not just his hand at mine, not just the warmth of his body, but his scent, his world, all wrapped around me like a manteau.

Sweeping down the hallway, I took delight in the smallest of things: flecks of paint on the linen wallpaper, the row of miniatures hung by hooks in the hall. I brushed fingers along a stack of books teetering on a hall table, then passed them, through the opened double doors at the end of the way. What might have been a dining room in another row house was a gallery in this one. A stained canvas covered the floor, and painted ones sat in stacks against the wall.

"Please, Amelia," Nathaniel said, catching up to me and staying me with a hand on my shoulder. What a monster I was, to enjoy discomfiting him so. "Let me take you home."

Instead, I slipped from beneath his touch. He had an easel at the window, and I wanted to see what wonders he'd worked at it. And then I murmured a soft sound when I finally saw.

Once again, he'd put life in the art—water flowing as real water did, a diaphanous gown drifting on the surface of it. It was plainly meant to be Ophelia, drowned for want of Hamlet's love, but the face on the figure was mine.

"Is this . . ." I started, then turned to him. A curious cold drifted around me, no more so when Nathaniel refused to meet my eyes. Instead of speaking to him, I asked him directly in my mind. He would prove himself, for once, for all. *Is this your premonition for me?*

Nathaniel jerked his head back. "It's a painting. Nothing more."

Swallowing hard, I turned back to it, and this time I indulged. I reached out to touch the water and drew back an oily smear of blue and gray. When I rubbed it between my fingers, it melted away, until nothing but a shadowy stain remained. "I'm dead in it."

With that, he seemed to recover. "You're alive now. Follow me, Amelia."

Instead, I asked, "How do you hear me?"

"I listen."

Frustration stung, and I shook my head. "*How* do you hear me, Nathaniel? How is it that you're the only one in the flames who sees me?"

Holding out a hand to me, he drew me in. His cologne filled me, driving away all the primal, astringent scents of his studio.

His heat radiated through his shirt, and he tucked my head beneath his chin. "I think sometimes each of the elements breathes life into a particular body. You seem very like fire to me."

I rested my cheek against his chest. I listened to his human heart. "What would that make you?"

"Come on," he said, and took my hand.

❋ ❋ ❋

As we ran through the park, I spun around, turning my gaze to the monument thrust against the sky. A marble column soared above my head, glowing with unusual luminance.

At the top, our first president pointed serenely toward the harbor. In this late and glimmering hour, he seemed a part of the heavens.

Nathaniel stopped beside me, his eyes turned toward the marvel as well. Deliberately, accidentally, I could never say for certain, his knuckles grazed against mine as he murmured, "You can see the whole of the city from the top."

"Would that I could," I said. The air had turned thick, breathing it an exercise.

Turning only eyes to me, Nathaniel said, "Stand a moment, then follow me directly." And then he stepped off.

I watched him move across the marble walk, his strange, rolling gait nevertheless silent, even as I concentrated all my attention on each fall of his feet. I let him go so long, he threw a look over his shoulder to find me.

How quickly I'd come to savor those glimpses of his vulnerability, those tiny proofs that my heart was not the only heart that faltered. I swooped down on those tender scraps, viciously glad to devour them. I wondered at myself that his distress should please; what was the matter with me?

Would that I were goodhearted; would that I wished all the best, selfless things for him—but I didn't. Stripping him of his defenses in Annapolis had softened me. Once he was vulnerable, I could curl in his arms—I could surrender a kiss and all my senses to him.

With deliberation, I straightened, then followed directly as commanded. But I followed in my own time, no more hurried than I would be if strolling the park come Sunday. Regal in my procession, I let my fingers admire the black iron gate as I passed it.

Nathaniel reached out of the darkness to grab me. He pulled me by gentle force into the monument's foyer, pressing me against the wall, so close I could taste the hot fall of his breath on my mouth. "Did you come only to torment me?"

Slipping beneath his arm, I dashed to the foot of a spiral staircase, turning my eyes up to get lost in the whorls as I mounted the steps. I laughed and said, "Not *only* to torment you."

And with that, I lifted my hems and ran. Hardly fast, for neither gowns nor corsets, nor heels and narrow passages permitted an exceptional sprint—but fast enough. Fast enough to dare him and call him, bid him chase me and catch me if he could.

The sound of my flight clamored on the steps. It echoed up and down, bouncing on marble from every direction, until the sound of it seemed as great as the roar of the ocean, as the pounding of my pulse in my ears. I cried out, a sharp laugh, a sharp scream, all melted into one when he got close enough to drop fingers on my shoulder.

Spinning in the narrows, I stumbled and would have fallen back onto the steps, but he caught me around the waist. He knew no shame, going about without gloves, but I blessed him, for I could feel the fever in his touch without them. Above, gasping for my breath, I gazed on him.

He turned his face up to me. I could have knighted or executed him in that moment, with him bended at my knee. Instead, I sank into his gaze. A distant rhythm of thunder swept through his voice when he asked, "Are you mine now?"

Shamelessly, I let him steal closer, I let him think he'd won my kiss. At the moment before the embrace, I hauled myself up forcibly and fled up the stairs. My laughter rose with the roar of the steps, with his cursing below. I flew like a hawk; I felt lifted on wings.

The landing came too soon. I caught myself on an arch there and lost all my breath. For I *could* see all of Baltimore laid at my feet. A fearsome terror took me when I stepped onto the deck that circled the column.

Its rail came only to my knee—nothing stood between me and plunging to the fence-framed walks below. Then, from behind, arms looped round my waist as Nathaniel pulled me against his chest.

"Now you're caught, aren't you?" he murmured in my ear, and I turned like a wanton toward the sound of his voice.

I could catch but a glimpse of him over my shoulder, a crescent curve of his moon face. The black fan of his lashes lowered, and his lips parted, painted dusky in the dark. I had no answer for him—I had no words at all.

The wind stole my longing for cruel delights. I wanted

nothing but to live there — in the gentle cage of his embrace — always and ever.

Turning on this precarious edge, I brushed my nose against his and blushed for trying to find myself in his eyes. I drew out, on hooks, a plaintive whisper. "I mustn't stay."

"Should I recite for you?" he asked. "Shakespeare, on parting with a kiss?"

Emboldened by his touch, fearless with the whole world beneath me, I said, "No. Speak *your* heart to me."

"I always do," Nathaniel said. He shifted, covering his arm with mine. As he brushed a kiss behind my ear, he laid my own hand on my breast, mapping me against his body. "In there, that's my heart. My breath."

Swept unsteady, I startled at the sweet pain that filled me. Since our first meeting, I ran mad with him; he ran wild in my veins. We had no quiet affection to spare between us, only tempting and taunting and impossible longings. I felt dashed on his shore, or that I was the stone on which he wrecked, and recklessly I said, "Tell me you love me."

He skimmed our joined hands to my throat, our mingled fingers touching the points of the setting sun on velvet. "Amelia."

"Tell me," I said, making a spiral in his arms, coming round to face him. Oh, and in that moment's dizziness, I felt the empty air behind me yawning, spreading out for me to fall through it, but I clutched Nathaniel's red coat and pressed into him. "Tell me you do, as you never have done."

Suddenly, the blackness of his eyes seemed very like the void that followed a crack of lightning. Something happened there, a steeling or a surrender, I couldn't tell which.

Deliberate, he traced my face, only this once, and let his gaze follow his fingers. They marked the curve of my brow, the hollow of my cheek, and so entranced was I by the prospect that he might line my lips, that I barely noticed the step he took forward—the step that propelled me back.

Just as he parted his lips to speak, I parted mine, but instead of a confession, he said, with the most exquisite weight to the words, "Jump with me."

Sixteen

F ROM BENEATH US, a wind came off the harbor, as if commanded. It pulled at my gown, my hair, whispering as it pulled ringlets loose and tossed them. It carried the spice of gardens in bloom, the sweet song of hoofbeats, the salty wake of the sea—the cool kiss of summer almost at an end. Dancing, pulling—swirling in eddies all around us, it beckoned.

Growing still, I searched Nathaniel's face for some evidence of amusement. I found none—I knew I would find none. Maybe I had none of his little details, no stolen glimpses of him at a washboard or playing cards, but I had his heart. His breath. And that soothed me.

I gave a glance at my skirts, then raised them enough to step onto the rail. Everywhere, I burned; I trembled—I had the most curious, perhaps hysterical sensation that the wind would take me off my feet and we would go flying, Nathaniel and I. That we could master this sky and disappear into it.

"Are you certain?" Nathaniel asked. He offered my escape as easily as he would offer to fill my glass, and when I nodded, he stepped onto the railing beside me. The wind came up again, mussing the waves of his hair. How queer that none should see us, that none of those citizens scurrying as ants below should call out.

We stood there, silhouetted against white marble, gazing out at a harbor town grown large. How many little houses there were; how many lives lived there on the shores of the Chesapeake.

Tightening my hand in Nathaniel's, I closed my eyes to all of it and said, "Shouldn't I be afraid?"

"Let me tell you, Amelia," he replied, "as I've told no other."

His arms came round me, and we slipped off the rail, plunging into a gold and glimmering dark. It wound around us as a cloak, swallowing sound and light, even the furious pull of gravity, and then, with a jolt, it lifted.

Stumbling like a wet foal, I held my arms out wide. I opened my eyes to the yard behind the Stewarts' house.

I whipped around and fell into Nathaniel's arms, prickling numb everywhere. This could be neither heaven nor hell, for flames licked not at our heels, and Mrs. Stewart's voice, carried out the window as she fixed a homely dinner, was surely no angelsong.

"What . . . how did you do this?" I asked, though I'm not sure I spoke the words.

All the same, he answered me. Curling his knuckle beneath my chin, he said, "How do you see the future?"

The ground seemed to move beneath my feet, as if I'd stepped from a ship after a long voyage. "The sunset parts a curtain for me, nothing more. That's hardly the same as slipping the bonds of earth, how . . . you said you went on foot as any man!"

"I do!"

At once, I remembered his explanation for my ability. "Are you . . . do you think you're the air?!"

"Yes, I do," he said.

My mouth dropped open. Shock turned my head, and my thoughts clamored. So many at once, I could barely sort them. Finally, before he put a hand on me, I managed to demand, "Then how could you leave me waiting in Annapolis?"

"Water below the ground slows me. Rivers may as well be walls." Nathaniel closed into himself, adding with a defensive tilt to his gaze. "And it was the truth that I couldn't afford my share of the cab."

Trembling, I reached for my pendant. "Are you even a man?"

He closed on me, hands out, as if he couldn't quite bear the thought of touching me. "I'm no more and no less the thing you are. You see in the fire at day's end. I go on the wind. I wish you wouldn't look at me like that."

"Like what?"

"Miss Stewart's almost at the front door," he answered, taking my elbow. "Go on then, and catch up with her, before she gets inside. You won't be ruined on account of me. Not tonight, anyway."

Temper alight, I pulled my arm from him and snapped, "You cannot close yourself to me, Nathaniel! I will not be driven."

"You *can't* be driven—you're too inconstant," he said. Stalking out before me, he turned and gestured at his whole self. "You say to me, tell me you love me—"

"And you still haven't!"

"I gave you the one thing I have! The only thing I possess, owed no one, and no thing. Is that not token enough for you?"

Swallowed in the sudden heat of tears, I came toward him, making my voice low, for the lights had risen in two windows beside us. Zora's voice echoed from the street, her laughter carried on a breeze. "I only asked for words."

Weary, Nathaniel considered the yellow streaks spilling into the drive. Stepping carefully around them, to keep the shadows to him, he came toward me, but our time to argue or make endearments had died.

"I love you," he said, and before me he disappeared.

After dinner, after what seemed like every dish in the house needed washing, Zora and I finally retired upstairs.

We'd had little to say while we ate, for while the Stewarts knew we played at sendings and visions, they truly thought it playing. Mrs. Stewart called it my Eastward Parlor Trick and only laughed that it seemed to make us so popular.

Closing ourselves in our room came as a relief to me. I

felt as though I wore weights on my fingers instead of rings. My narrow slice of bed had never seemed so inviting.

"Did you find him?" Zora finally asked.

Shaking my head, I told her, "I'd rather not speak of it."

What a great crevasse that left between us, so I asked, "What did it look like when I slipped into my vision this afternoon? I felt as though I blinked, and it was over."

"It was very like that for us, too." She moved as if through water, peeling her layers one by one.

I left my wrapper at the foot of our bed. "Sometimes losing myself in the sight frightens me, but I'd rather have that a hundred times than . . . I can't begin to define it. I don't know what to call what happened today."

Zora moved around me, a pattern intricate as a quadrille that we'd learned bit by bit. I turned toward the desk, while she opened the armoire, closing the windows, and one-two-three-four.

"Writing, I suppose." Zora started the work of unclasping all her hooks. "That's all it seemed to us."

"Not particularly crazed?"

She offered an apologetic smile and shook her head. "Dull, really. Like watching Joey Dobbs work his figures on the board."

That slice of ordinary made me laugh; Zora made me laugh, and I felt the worst guilt at holding my tongue with her. The last thing I should have hoped for her was to lay my own troubles on her shoulders. "How is Thomas?"

"Horrified at you," she said, but she took the edge from the answer with a smile. She hung her wrapper inside the armoire, then turned to lean back against it. "Would you think I've gone mad if I said that the longer I know him, the fonder I become?"

"I thought you already quite fond."

"This is something else entirely. It's not just the spark that jumps out of the fire." Then, blushing, she hurried to add, "That's there yet. Oh, I'm making a mess of this."

Sitting heavily on the bed, I heard something hit the floor. As I pulled my skirts up to search, I said, "You are, indeed, for I haven't the first idea what you're getting at."

Zora swept down suddenly, rooting on the floor, and as I looked at her dark head, she told me, "I like listening to him. His philosophies, and he listens to mine . . ."

"Do you have even one?" I asked. "It's the first you've mentioned it to me."

Slapping my knee with a glove, she rose and shoved it in my hands. "A great many of them, thank you. And the point

I'm trying hard to make—in spite of your endless interruptions—"

With a cheeky grin, I said, "Am I interrupting? I apologize."

Zora flung herself back toward the armoire, raising her voice as if to beat me with it. "I feel as though each time I see him, we become something greater. More ourselves than we've ever been."

I smiled, swallowed up in her sentiment—cloaking myself in it, I suppose, to forget my own upset. "Zora Stewart, have you fallen in love with the doctor's son?"

"I think I have." With a great sigh, Zora sank to sit on the armoire bench. Then, shaking herself back to sense, she held out her hand. "Give me your gloves, I'm right here."

Reaching into my pocket, I pulled out two, which, curiously, left me with a third. With the extra in hand, I turned it backwards and fore, shaking my head. "This isn't mine."

"You little thief." Zora's smile twisted in admiration. "You made your own prediction come true!"

In running mad, I'd forgotten entirely the line that had incensed our hostess so—*In the vespers, I see this lovely glove of crêpe and kid, gone missing and ruining the set.* The thing must have fallen into the layers of my polonaise—how miraculous that it could have stayed there across the city by carriage and magic alike.

"My mystic eye is never wrong," I said, pretending dramatics like Privalovna. Watching Zora pet the glove as if it were a curious artifact from the sands of Egypt, I couldn't help but laugh.

※ ※ ※

When the storms came to Baltimore, they painted it with a laden, gray brush. Though thunder rippled across the sky, it was no furious peal; it had no lightning to decorate it. It was the sort of storm that wrapped a day in cotton, blunting mind and mood to a singular, dreary state.

I stood at the back door, trying to tempt some of the cooling mist into a kitchen sweltering with all-day baking, but none came. Somewhere in this, Zora sat with a sick aunt, no doubt enjoying her visit as much as I enjoyed my lack of one, which was to say, not at all. I had it on good authority that this aunt smelled of camphor and onions.

"Plenty to do if you've run out of your own errands," Mrs. Stewart told me. Elbow deep in bread dough with the downstairs girl, she cut me a practical look. "You're slowing down my rise, letting the wind in like that."

"Sorry," I murmured, closing the door and leaning back against it. "I could help, if you like."

Mrs. Stewart shook her head, and I noticed for the first time the fine, silver streaks shot through her hair. "Got four elbows in here already. Take some lace to mend; you've got a pretty hand."

"Thank you," I said, groaning inwardly. Patently foolish to ask for a chore and then regret getting one, but so it was. I picked up the sewing basket on my way from the kitchen, thinking to settle in the foyer, where the light was good.

"Have you ever seen such a fine day?" Mr. Stewart joked. He sat in the little chair by the window, the one I'd meant to take.

"It's handsome, indeed," I answered, carrying on to the parlor, where I could smell the rain vividly, mixed with a bit of ash. As I settled near the fireplace, I shivered. The wind whistled down the chimney, offering a chill more spiritual than physical.

How funny that I should find the cries of Maryland wind so disconcerting. The screams a nor'easter made had driven any number of hearty souls from Maine; I enjoyed them, in my own way.

But then, nothing but snow came on that wind, did it?

My heart caught in a painful twist. Pulling lace from the sewing basket, I fixed my attention on its net. I bade myself think of needles and thread, of closing broken strands, of naught more. But fixing lace was no strenuous task. My fingers knew it uncommanded; they gave my thoughts leave to wander.

What could I make of myself? I was, in part, fearsomely delighted that so much water in the wind would keep Nathaniel from coming to me. Then, the next part wept in agony over the same.

Rent in two, I saw neither clearly nor completely my whole—for how could I want him and wish him away at once? My country concerns of becoming a good woman and making a good match had been abandoned to the tempest entirely. To the elements.

Pricking through the lace and into my flesh, I frowned and stuck the finger in my mouth. To keep from staining it, or because I had no genuine wish to mend it, I dropped the lace into the basket again and laid my head in the curl of my arms, right on the table.

I stirred my lazy fingers through the box of calling cards. Picking out one, I listlessly admired the script printed there, then dropped it on the table. Reaching in for another, I drew out yet another strawberry pink card, and I smiled, unsurprised that the sugar heiress had called again.

I'd seen two gentlemen in shirtsleeves fighting on a lawn for her, and as she was society, I'd had the pleasure of reading that prediction come true in the *Sunpapers*. Scandal at the Sugarcane Ball! A photograph of the heiress in question had shown her exquisitely pleased in place of horrified.

Dropping that card, I fished for another. *Pour présenter,* a stranger to me, so I moved to the next. Caleb's card, Mattie's card—one from an older lady whom I'd seen come into money, a note writ on the back to thank me—as if the windfall would come from my purse and not some distant relation. That card fluttered from my fingers as I reached for another, and another still. Little victories and mysteries in that box, all of my making, or soon would be.

Weary with myself, I reached in one last time. Thomas' card came up, and my heart warmed. I had never known it before, how the glow of someone else's joy could reflect so completely as to be shared.

Skimming my thumb across the deep-set engraving of his name, I smiled to myself as a faint band of gold slipped through the window.

"Amelia," Mr. Stewart said, shaking me.

With a jerk, I looked up, the thinnest veil of a headache come over me. "Yes, sir?"

"Dinner's nearly ready. You might clean up that mess before Mrs. Stewart sees it." He made a face for me, pretending to cut his finger across his throat. Always his eyes laughed and danced, and he whistled merrily as he went off.

Pushing the chair back, I gazed at all the calling cards spread on the table. Instead of an ungainly heap, they sat face-down in columns, arranged four across. Face-down, indeed, but the verso sides had my writing on them now. A little pencil rolled away as I stood, as I leaned over to read helplessly.

In a family way, I'd written on the back of a pink card I had no need to reverse to identify. *Boarding a ship,* said the next—that card belonged to Caleb. *New dress torn, carriage wheel broken, winning at poker.* All these fates in three and four words—they horrified me, for I had not the first memory of marking them.

And yet they amazed me.

The whole of a life pared to a scrawl on the back of a calling card, one moment belonging alone to time—and to me.

Short a penny, riding a train, I read, turning cards faster to match their fortune with their name. *Mother of twins, falling down stairs.* I didn't even think to tremble when I came to the last, I was only greedy to read it, to match it, *Dead by September*. Daring myself, I flipped it.

MR. THOMAS REA
DIVISION STREET

The front door slammed, and Zora called out, "Rain's stopped a bit!"

Panic seized me but not in stillness. I scrambled to shove Thomas' card into my basque, then hurried to clear the rest before Zora caught a glimpse of any of it. Destroying the neat columns, I swept all the cards into their box, and I cursed the cold fireplace, for if I could have, I would have burned the whole lot.

"How pale you are," Zora said, flicking water from her manteau toward me. Then her gaze dropped and her bemused smile faltered. "Are you bleeding?"

"It's only a pinprick," I said, and fled up the stairs.

The rain poured on and on outside; it caressed the window in whispering rivulets, subtle percussion on the roof of the house. In our upstairs room, we heard it best, and though I had much heavy on my mind, I found I had to fight the pull of sleep.

"Do you know," I told Zora, looking over my shoulder at her, "I think it's funny that I've never looked for you or Thomas."

She hummed softly. Heels bumping mine, she didn't roll over, but she did turn her face up to be heard. "I wouldn't want to know. You saw Nella's wedding day, and now she'll anticipate it until it finally arrives."

"Is that so terrible?"

At that, Zora did roll over. She winced to find herself too close to my face, covering her nose with her hand and shifting back. "You smell of Mama's stewed cucumbers."

Sliding away from her, I said, "It's not just me."

Soft laughter shook the bed as Zora settled in again. Tucking her head in her arm, she tugged at the sheets as she mused aloud. "I want the wonder of it. I don't want to know that he *will* propose to me and impatiently wait for it to happen."

An ache bloomed in my chest. "You're not impatient now?"

"I'm not," Zora said, and she sounded as if she marveled a little at herself for it. "Truly, I'm not. Everything's extraordinary. And everything that isn't sweetens the rest."

The silver charm at my throat jabbed its points into my skin. "I'd want a warning for everything that isn't."

Slipping her fingers up between us, Zora pressed at a furrow I hadn't even realized I'd made in my brow. As if she could draw calm from the air, she smiled and rubbed at me until I settled. Pleased, she said, "Wasn't it the best dance, though? The first you danced after Nathaniel finally arrived?"

I rested my brow against her hand and sighed. "It really was."

"It's intolerable the way you moon. Do you want to talk about it tonight?" Zora pressed the bridge of my nose with her thumb, rather hard actually. "If you don't say anything, I'll only assume the worst and loathe him for you."

I rolled onto my back, better to gaze at the ceiling and betray nothing. If she would hear naught, I could warn Thomas instead. He'd take care, and all would be well. Banishing my thoughts on that, I sighed and said, "Don't loathe him. Or do. I run inconstant, or he is a monster—and I know not which."

"A monster?" Zora asked. She sounded more tickled than concerned. "I'm sorry, I don't mean to laugh, but everything's the end of the world for you two."

"You were ready to have me abandon him for being late to a dance," I reminded her.

Raising her hands above us, Zora swayed and swirled, miming the putting on of a ring. "Hardly! I was ready to have you abandon him for making you miserable when he's not even a good prospect! If you can't marry him, he should at least make you deliriously happy until the end."

Thunder rolled across the roof and across my skin. Very like the vibration from running up the monument, it stirred my memories. It was true—I found them much sweeter for the disaster that came after. Few could say they dared to leap so readily as I had, but I wondered if anyone should.

"Amelia?" Zora asked, rubbing her elbow against mine. "Are you there?"

"Only contemplating the end of the world, that's all."

"What did happen, then?"

With a great heave, I threw myself on my face and buried the answer in my pillow. "He asked me to jump, and I did." The whole bed shook when Zora rose up. Clapping her hands on my shoulders, she shook me until I had no choice but to roll to face her.

"You're making me mad with all this intrigue."

I clasped her arms to still her. "He loves me; I made him say it."

"And did *you* say it?" She seemed round as a soap bubble, impossibly full and fragile just then.

"No," I said, covering my face with my hands. "Tomorrow at the park, I might. Or I might not. Do you think I'm terrible with him?"

Zora rolled her eyes, impossibly lovely in her exasperation. "Essentially, yes. But you're terrible without him. May as well resign yourself to it."

"Am I really?"

"I'm going to take my two hands and smother you," Zora said, laughing. "Make up your mind!"

It was oddly comfortable, knowing she thought I was foolish. I looked in fire and saw the future; Nathaniel went on the winds. Should we both be monsters or not, it seemed we were infinitely suited. Soothed with that balm, I said, "Easier if you made it for me!"

The great crash the bed made when Zora fell back in it again was the last provocation Mrs. Stewart needed. In the room below, she thumped her ceiling. "Enough, you circus monkeys!"

Zora giggled and kept her tongue just a moment, then rolled toward me again to whisper in my ear, "If you should elope, tell me. Thomas and I will come and make it double."

A sickness seeped into my chest again, but I forced a smile and said, "I shall, I promise."

Seventeen

BECAUSE OF THE RAINS, we couldn't lounge so lei-surely at the park. We flocked like birds, standing on the walk as we took our turns at the bow, then hurrying back to shake our hems dry.

"I've only got six now!" Sarah scowled at Zora as she bounded off to retrieve yet another lost arrow.

Disappearing into the brush, Zora called back, "It's not lost yet!"

"You know," I told Sarah. "If you married a man with a good trade, you should be able to afford all the arrows you like. You could have them instead of pins for your hair."

Agitated as she paced the walk, Sarah swung round to

face me. "It pleases me to know that I bought my own arrows, thank you."

"With the pennies you got for your birthday," Mattie
said, then added, "When she was ten. They're ancient,
you know."

Mattie kept her laughter very quiet and confidential between us. More resilient than I'd credited her for, she took
the most darling delight in watching our sportswomen
bicker between shots. Mainly, I did the job of holding the
quiver. Though I had taken a shot or two, I didn't buck to
have my turn next. Unlike Zora, I knew I was rather
bad at it.

"Oy," someone called, flouting all good manners, and we
three turned toward the voice. Caleb raised his hand and
strode toward us like he'd been invited. Though he stopped
close to Sarah, he looked out at the target. "Still pulling to
the left, I see."

"That's Mattie's shot," Sarah said.

"Oh," Caleb replied, as if placating her.

Heat flashed in Sarah's eyes, and she squared her shoulders. "I should like to see you best me."

Bounding out of the trees, Zora thrust her hand above
her head in triumph. "Didn't I tell you I'd find it?"

"Brilliant," Sarah said. She lifted her skirts and stalked

out to her spot before the target. I offered an arrow and a murmured wish of best luck.

On a full draw, Sarah looked so like a huntress goddess that it rather left me awestruck. I saw her take the breath she'd once advised me, before setting the arrow to flight. When it struck the heart of the centermost circle, her divinity fell away, and she whooped.

Clapping gleefully, Mattie cried, "Amazing!"

"You should call it a draw before you embarrass yourself," Zora told Caleb, hiding a smile.

With a sweet, mocking nod, Sarah offered Caleb the bow. "If it pleases you, Mr. Grey, could you show me how to improve my aim?"

"Oh!" Zora grabbed my elbow and started to pull me away.

"Have care," I said. "I've been mending lace a week now!"

"Our beaux are here," Zora answered, and I stopped caring about my lace entirely.

When I turned, my heart leaped to see the god-awful tartan of Nathaniel's jacket even before I saw him. The gold and green, despite the gilt and greenness of the summer season in Druid Hill Park, stood out.

With a giddy sort of relief, I decided that I might be inconstant after all, but when I smiled, he smiled, and I no longer cared if we might be monsters.

"We're astonished to find you here," Thomas told Zora with a smile. "Mr. Witherspoon came about this morning, and our only thought was to take in some sunshine lest it should rain again."

Slipping his hand into mine, Nathaniel added, "It was only a feeling I had, that this end of the park might make for more pleasant sightseeing."

The surge of my pulse left me near lightheaded, but it beat out apologies, mine to him, his to me, and I was only sorry now that we stood on a public walk. Two clasped hands, however scandalous, couldn't fulfill me for a reconciliation.

"Miss Holbrook is teaching Mr. Grey a lesson in humility," Zora said, gesturing back at our party.

"That's the measure of a man's affection," Nathaniel said, hooking his finger inside my glove. He should have let go once we met—but then, there were a great many things Nathaniel and I should have done, that we never did.

"His keenness to prostrate himself before her?" Zora asked.

Scratching across my wrist, Nathaniel offered Zora a twisted smile. "And her avid desire to see it."

"I don't think it's necessary," Thomas said, and though we found the ground quite firm and certain beneath us, he put a hand on Zora's back as if to guide her over rough terrain. It seemed even the most gentlemanly of our circle could be coaxed into duplicity, and how charming he was at it.

"It's not," I said. Taking my hand from Nathaniel, I met his black eyes and offered my elbow instead. "That's the great appeal."

"Mad with power," Nathaniel said. His murmurs slipped into me, onto me, warming me in his familiar way. If he knew my thoughts, he knew my wanton, wilding desire to hide away with him. Longing felt like a thread, slipping between us, sewing us together.

Zora glanced over her shoulder. "Quite sensible with it, I think."

Coming back to the contest at hand, Mattie returned the quiver to me and fluttered on the edges of our party. "Isn't it exciting?"

"Wildly," I said, but I could barely see Caleb draw his next shot.

I kept closing my eyes—as if I could will Nathaniel to carry us with the wind again. My few days' vacillation disappeared. Standing on his arm, taking the heat of his gaze, I knew if he asked it again, I would jump.

A hundred times, I would jump.

"The wind kicked up," Caleb complained as he squelched across wet earth to rejoin us. He held the bow out for Sarah but didn't release it to her grasp. Instead, he made her tug it, his nose crinkling at the little play of war before she wrested it away.

"I think the only wind about us," she said, as she turned to me for an arrow, "is the great hot one you're blowing."

"Oh, cruel," I said, handing her a feathered shaft. Mattie laughed and wrapped herself around my free arm, resting her chin on my shoulder. When Sarah took her position again, Mattie whispered to me, "Would you like to hear a secret?"

"Always."

"Caleb asked her hand." Mattie smiled and sighed, trying to sway with me, but Nathaniel kept me quite firmly grounded on the other side. I felt rather like a door, waving on a hinge between them.

"What did she say?"

"Ask again next week."

I laughed, but before I could ask more, a crack rent the air. A ripple ran through us, and Caleb cried out. He rushed across the lawn and was nearly on Sarah when I realized that she'd crumpled to the ground, letting the bow fall where it may.

• 251 •

A halo of gold passed before my eyes, and I felt the weakness in Sarah's knees as she staggered and stood. I looked into my hands, and then pulled Mattie to me, hiding her from that next thing she would see.

Without the glimmer of sunset, the blood that spilled through Sarah's gloves only shocked.

"Bring her, Caleb," Thomas said, suddenly commanding. A center of calm in this storm, he turned to Zora and told her, "Run! Fetch her parents!"

Sweeping Sarah into his arms, Caleb dared any to say something against it. Zora took Mattie by the hand, dragging her in the opposite direction. Only Nathaniel and I hesitated, and we had a silent argument. *Can't you do something? Can't you take her faster?*

The shadow on his brow was his reply; he could but he couldn't. *How to explain disappearing, reappearing? How to explain being in one place, then somewhere else in an instant?*

"Yours is a parlor trick," he said aloud, his face ashen. "Mine could be witchcraft."

Nodding, I backed away. He did, too, widening the gulf between us. Then, at the same moment, we turned. I would follow Zora to deliver bad news; Nathaniel would follow Thomas and Caleb to offer only his strength.

For two so gifted as we, how utterly useless we were.

❊ ❊ ❊

Though the news concerned our friend and cousin, Zora's parents kept it from us in whispers. Notes came, and then neighbors—each time, Mrs. Stewart sent us upstairs to work our samplers. Never had we cared so little about stitching our names in floss, and rarely had we so flagrantly disregarded Mrs. Stewart's command. Once voices started in the kitchen again, we crept in stocking feet to the top of the stairs.

"And to happen to such a pretty girl," Mrs. Stewart told someone, for the third time at least. Zora had started to lose her temper at it, and I stayed her with a hand. We wouldn't find out anything if she tore down there in a rage.

"Dr. Rea said she can have a glass one," a woman said, casually, as if discussing a new lamp furnace. "Enamel's the best, but too expensive."

"Ghastly. Perhaps we could take a collection?"

Zora surged beneath my hand again. "Would they wound her twice? Bad enough her eye, but her pride, too, treating her to charity?"

"They mean well," I said.

"It's all well-meaning," Zora said, collapsing on the step in frustration. Tears streaked down her cheeks. The narrow stairs closed around us, dark and warm, almost like a chapel. Pulling her sleeves over her hands, she swiped at her face. "You know her, Amelia. What of her prospects now?"

I sank to sit beside her. "Caleb wants to marry her."

With a dismayed groan, Zora waved me away. "Who knows if he really means it?"

"He does. He asked her."

"She didn't say anything." Sniffling, Zora rubbed her fingers beneath her red nose, too ladylike, at least, to wipe that with her sleeve. "Did you see it?"

Shaking my head, I leaned against the wall. "Mattie told me."

"Then that should be the thing to cheer her," Zora said, though she didn't sound like she meant it.

"I've never understood, precisely, what Caleb and Sarah are to each other," I admitted, for I couldn't quite believe it, either. "They sparkle and crack, but she's always refusing to admit him—what is that?"

A silence of immeasurable weight stretched between us. Then, softly, Zora said, "You must never repeat this."

Cold banded me, and I nodded. "I vow."

"He ruined her," she said, so low I had to lean to catch her words. "They've barbed each other since they were babes, and summer last, it spilled over. We'd gone to the beach for a clambake, and nightfall, and atmosphere, and the caves nearby . . ."

Shocked, I swear, I felt all my blood drain out at once. "He forced himself on her?"

"No!" Zora shut her mouth, listening to see if we'd accidentally called attention to ourselves. When the conversation below continued, so did she. "He called and she answered. It was a lapse, and no one knows it. But *they* know. He wants her hand, and she wants a choice in the matter."

Oh, how sharp that admission felt, pulling between my ribs. "But what sense does it make to refuse him if she wants him?"

Her smile starting to quaver again, Zora gathered herself and stood. She had her own fondness, her own memories, and quite plainly Sarah's maiming had struck a deep wound in her as well. It took a moment for Zora to still her breath, and even then the threat of tears came in her voice. But she managed, at last, to answer me.

"None. It makes no sense at all."

"She refused me," Mattie said, turning and turning her tea-cup but never lifting it to drink. She seemed almost of paper, not just pale, but easily creased as well. "So I hoped if we should all call together, she'd change her mind."

"I'd like that," I said.

Managing a bit of wan sympathy, Mattie turned her cup again and said, "You must feel such guilt."

Tea went bitter on my tongue. "We all do, I suppose."

"But you saw it," Mattie said. Her eyes strayed toward mine, each blink slow as surrender. "And handed her the arrow that did it, besides."

The kitchen walls seemed to close on us. Suddenly, the heat from the stove became unbearable, burning all the air from the room—at least, that's how it felt to me. Trying not to rattle my cup on its saucer, I looked from Zora to Mattie and said, "But I wasn't the cause of it."

"Oh, I know." A mirthless smile touched her lips, an attempt at etiquette and nothing more.

Zora stood to gather our dishes. Briskly, much in the mode of her mother, she said, "Let's take her a pot of ginger apples."

"I'll go pick some if you scrape the ginger," I told Mattie, already at the back door. A rude hostess, indeed, I didn't wait for her reply. I just hurried into the yard, suddenly breathing again once I'd escaped the kitchen.

Ducking beneath the heavy arms of the tree that shaded the yard, I rose in its bower, hidden away for just a moment. The earth smelled dark and rich around me, teased at my feet with the sharp hint of fermented apples, and sweet in a haze around my head with the promise of still-ripening ones. Bees hummed as they ate their fill, and sunshine, pure and clean, slipped in sparks through the leaves above.

"Nathaniel," I said, pulling my polonaise out to catch the apples I picked. "Do you hear me?"

The wind answered, the slightest rush to tug at my hair. I pulled another apple from its branch and called again — more in thoughts than voice. And on the third, I turned and he was there.

The branches shook sunlight across Nathaniel's face, and for once no impish humor lingered in him. Dressed out in a plain muslin shirt and suspenders, he came across black and white, and strangely severe. When he stepped closer, he greeted me with the sharp scent of turpentine on his skin.

"I was working," he said.

A pang struck me anew that I still had no idea what it meant that Nathaniel did what he liked. Winter colors stained his skin, blues and grays and whites, and thoughtlessly I took his hand to examine it. "What are you making?"

"A pietà," he said. Then deliberately he rubbed a cerulean stain into my lace sleeve, making a permanent mark of himself there. Abandoning his distraction to consume me with a look, he pulled me against his chest. "You're troubled."

With a sigh, I laid my head on his shoulder. "Sarah won't see anyone, and everyone's unsettled."

Impossibly close, Nathaniel pressed his brow against my temple. "Aren't you?"

"No, I am, but I can scarcely call my distress as great as theirs. They've known her such a long time, and I, such a short one." I longed to bury my face against his neck, to feel his skin warm on mine. "And I've disturbed you only to send you home again. I only came out to pick apples."

Nathaniel carefully caught my hand and raised it to his lips. He didn't kiss; instead, he caressed, tracing across his mouth with both our hands, then set me free. "If a minute or an hour, I would always come for you."

"I should have told you before," I said, filled with his tender sentiment and a rush of my own. "That I love you, too."

Stepping into a blaze of light, Nathaniel smiled at me crookedly. "Go on, then."

"What?"

"You didn't say it before. Will you now?"

In spite of myself, I laughed, turning away from him, then turning back, just to taste the shock of heat that rose brand-new to my skin, on looking at him again. Pressing myself against him, I gazed into him and said into him, with my mouth and my mind, "I love you, too."

To answer, he leaned as if to kiss me and dissipated. He wasn't even a cool breath on my lips—simply there, then gone. And that made me laugh, too, the odd, glorious secret we shared and more so—knowing he would suffer for want of that unfinished embrace as well.

Ducking beneath the branches again, I surfaced in the yard and took two steps to find Mattie staring at me. I had never realized just how pale came the blue of her eyes, not until that moment, when light slanted into them, illuminating them like pools.

"The ginger's grated," she said. She had no guile to her, just a frigid stiffness.

"I've got apples." I lifted my polonaise in uneasy reply.

She very nearly let me by, but at the last caught my elbow. "I thought I heard laughter in the yard."

"It must have been the wind," I said.

And truly, was that a lie?

Eighteen

A GREAT CRY WENT UP in Eutaw Place that morning. One that seemed to go on endlessly, echoing in agonies that spread from house to house as a plague. It reached our doorstep in the shape of Thomas Rea, whose countenance came so gray we thought he might expire at the door.

"I need your father," he told Zora, brushing past her as he had never done, his eyes this once in search of someone besides his beloved. "I'm sorry to call so early."

Grasping his arms, Zora tried to catch him and keep him. "Thomas, what's the matter?"

"I need your father," he repeated. He pulsed with low urgency, and all but leaped at Mr. Stewart when he came around from the kitchen. Pulling him aside, he stole glances toward us, then had the gall to lower his voice.

Zora trembled beside me, clutching the ribbons of her housedress and skittering up two steps with me when her mother appeared and joined the frantic conversation in the hall.

"Oh, mercy," Mrs. Stewart said, then became her brusque self again, pushing both gentlemen to the door. "Breakfast can wait. I'll save a plate in the warmer, go on, go on."

Thomas apologized again and threw one thin and anxious look in Zora's direction as he opened the door. But he said nothing to her. Neither did Mr. Stewart, who put his best coat over his shirtsleeves and left the house without a wink or a jest or even a smile.

The moment the door closed, Zora and I spilled into the parlor.

"Mama!" Zora cried, our bare feet clapping against the kitchen floor. "Mama, what's all this?"

Mrs. Stewart turned from the basin, smoothing wet hands over her face. There could be no mistake that she'd tried to blanch away tears. Her eyes were already red with them, her voice thick. "Sarah's taken a turn."

A cold, iron bolt set my spine. "Is she ill?"

When her mother said nothing, Zora slapped a hand on

the table. The sharp sound startled all of us, for a ripple passed between us as Zora asked, "Mama, is she ill?"

"It's a terrible pain she's been in," Mrs. Stewart said. Gathering herself, she held a hand out to take Zora in. Yet she spoke not, not until I had come into her arms as well. I trembled on the edge of crying now, just knowing that no good could come of this.

"Please just say it, Mama."

"The bottle said two tablespoons," Mrs. Stewart said. All ragged hell played in her voice, catching and clicking as she tried to wheeze out the rest of it. "She took it all."

Zora cried out, a raw pain that ground into the bones. She clutched her mother's gown, sobbing into her shoulder. Grief so took her that she swayed the three of us. Every cry rocked into me, every heaving, gasping breath reverberated across my skin.

"She doesn't suffer anymore," Mrs. Stewart said, emotion unraveling her again.

In my numb horror, I stood still and stiff, as if I could escape an awful truth by hiding from it. But an awareness crept on me, a black thought winding like miasma to cloud my mind. I forced myself to speak, asking rather than guessing, because I prayed to be wrong. "What use is a lawyer to any of them?"

Some of Mrs. Stewart's sternness returned. Slowly, carefully, she answered, for it was a direct question she could hardly dismiss. "Emily Holbrook's sent for the police. She says the prescription is to blame."

"Oh, my poor Thomas," Zora cried, dissolving again. "His father is all he has!"

Quickly, I wrapped my arms around Zora from behind. I wanted to be there to catch her, to squeeze her, to carry her to the ground when the poisoned thought that rose to my mind spilled from Mrs. Stewart's lips.

"They're coming for Thomas, my duck. He wrote the prescription."

❄ ❄ ❄

As if mocking our tragedy, the sky refused to give up its startling clarity for mourning or burying. It relented not when the white crêpe was hung to signify her death nor as our procession carried us through the heart of the city to Greenmount Cemetery.

Summer seemed determined to see Sarah Holbrook buried in her own colors: golden, bronze, blue.

Though I was family in abstract, I was only barely so. Thus, once we left our carriage, I let Zora go with her parents to the front and humbly excused myself to the back. I would have ample chance to give my regrets—but it was none my place to do it before even a single relation.

When I finally did reach the casket, I laid my pretty bundle of delphiniums among the rest and pressed a kiss to the pewter plate that read *At Rest*. With a fortifying breath, I made myself look into the window above it. All those who said a body in death looked very like that dear friend in life spoke in lies.

Though I recognized Sarah's face, it was quite clear she no longer lived behind it. They had disguised her well, turning her face away to hide her wound, fitting her with a veiled hat to wear for eternity. But she seemed almost melted. Not so much as to be deformed, but distinctly pulled toward the ground that would soon embrace her.

Hurrying away, I couldn't be surprised when Nathaniel came to stand beside me. It was a voiceless comfort, without a sideward glance even in greeting—a single mark to prove I stood not entirely alone. Stripped of all color and gesture, we simply rested very near each other.

But even that drew attention. Caleb, in his black hat band, and rummy as the rest of the pallbearers, took sight of us and interrupted the hymn.

"Why don't you cry, Miss van den Broek?" Even across

uncertain ground, and reeking of whiskey, Caleb walked fine and straight—and right to me. "Have your tears all been used up?"

The blood in my veins thinned, running hot and fast. Clinging to my composure, I said, low, "Caleb, please."

A tight and furious beast, Caleb stalked to me directly. "Surely you've had time aplenty to grieve, given your *talents.*"

He spat that word at me. Beside me, Nathaniel hardened, but I splayed my hand, brushing his, warning him back. If Caleb ran his rawness out, then it would be done, and no more harm could come of it.

Swallowing to clear my throat, I whispered to him, "I am so sorry for your loss."

"Are you laughing?" Caleb threw up his hands, very like a ringmaster. My hope dissipated when he raised his voice, letting it carry above all assembled. There could be no ignoring the disturbance now. "Witness, everyone, the culmination of a prophet's wit!"

Nathaniel stepped in, reaching for Caleb to still him. "You've come undone in your grief, sir. I beg you come with me."

"Who are *you* to me?" Caleb shoved Nathaniel aside. Then he turned to me. Clamping hard hands on my arms, he seemed oblivious to the gasp risen up behind him—and, truth, I feared the crowd's shock would not save me.

Caleb shook me hard. "Aren't you clever, Miss van den Broek, that you promised nothing, and no *thing* this is, indeed! Do you laugh at me?!"

"I don't, I never—Caleb, I'm sorry!"

Nathaniel crashed into Caleb, sending them both in a black tumble to the ground. My sobs turned to a scream, the imprint of hard hands upon me aching, every muscle in my body begging to collapse. In the chaos, I couldn't tell where one fist began, where the other ended.

At last, they both terminated when Wills and Mr. Stewart pulled them apart. Caleb twisted as a rabid dog in Wills' arms, heaving with hard breath. Wiping blood from his mouth, Nathaniel murmured something to Mr. Stewart and made as if to walk away.

Incensed, Caleb rose up like vengeance. Breaking from Wills' grasp, he struck once more, visiting his retribution on me. Oblivious to all, he ripped my lace sleeves and threw me down. Against the burning sky, he towered over me.

Instinctively, I cowered against a blow I expected to come. Instead, this shadow spat at the ground and asked, "Are you laughing now?"

Through my tears, I couldn't make out the men who

dragged him off. And I barely knew that it was Nathaniel and another unknown to me who helped me to my feet. I swayed there, tattered and ashamed, burning under horrified scrutiny. I cast a look into the crowd to find one friendly face, or to at least make my first apologies to Zora, but I stopped in the middle of them, burned by blue eyes that, without tears, simply stared.

A scarlet flush touched Mattie's cheeks, and then she turned away in silence.

"I wish you'd stop apologizing," Zora said. She looked into the armoire, distracted as though she had come to it in search of something but couldn't recall what.

Of course, I knew, and gently I brushed her aside to take out my cambric walking suit. It felt unreasonably heavy in my arms; it took great effort to lay it on the bed to be folded. By reflex, I replied, "I'm sorry," then shook my head. "Hand me the paper, would you?"

Lost as she searched the room, Zora finally came upon the tissue in the chair and offered it to me. "I shouldn't know what to do with myself, now that you're going."

"It's almost a week yet you have me."

Zora sighed. "Such that it is."

Though yet another apology rose to my lips, I swallowed it. Folding the checked polonaise, I said instead, "I'm sorry I can't stay."

The emptiness played endlessly between us. With the funeral done, Zora still moved as if beneath water, restlessly to the window, and then to the armoire again, making herself busy with walking. I wore myself out laying gowns, then paper, then gowns again in my trunk.

A tap came at the door, and Mrs. Stewart let herself in. Even she had been hollowed—though she stood straight, yes, I could not imagine this woman pleasantly threatening a dock boy or driving her victoria like a charioteer.

"I thought you might want these as souvenirs," she said. She held up the box of calling cards, and then put it beside my trunk. Slipping out again, she pulled the door only hard enough to make it bounce against the jamb, leaving it ajar in her wake.

Zora reached into the box. "Alexis Stafford," she read, then added quietly. "I don't believe we ever had the chance to call on her."

"I don't remember."

"I know we never saw this one, Juniper Quisling? What an odd name."

The shape and sound of that teased my ear. A brief, vague flash struck me, *Burned by oil*, and I raised Zora's hand to look at the back of the card. There, my handwriting confirmed my memory, a three-word prediction scribbled in pencil as a storm parted.

"What?" Zora asked, then turned the card over. Her eyes widened.

Pressing her lips together, she pulled another card from the box, reading one side, then the other. When she did, I hurried to the armoire, for that box was short a card, one I'd slipped first into my polonaise and then into an accidentally stolen glove.

I couldn't be sure how many cards she had read as I stood there with Thomas' in my hands. I only knew—I only wondered, did she mean it, truly, when she said she would have no future seen for her? Squeezing the glove tight, I crushed the card in my grip.

"When did you do this?" Zora asked.

"The afternoon when you sat in with your aunt," I said, turning around. "There's one missing from the lot."

"Just one?"

If it were any other day, it seemed she might be amused at the specificity. How I hated to ruin that, but how much more would I hate myself should this prediction bear out like the others—should I have known the number of her heart's days and hidden it from her.

"It's Thomas'. Would you have it?"

With a delicate touch, Zora steadied herself. "Will I like it?"

Heat spread cross my chest, burning beneath the charm that pricked at my throat. I wanted to say aloud, *No! No!* but I could only shake my head. Zora's figure smeared in my sight, and I fought hard to hold my tears. I couldn't cry. I wasn't entitled to cry, when I was that thing that caused the harm.

When she came toward me, I thought she meant to take it. Instead, she kissed my cheek, then squeezed my shoulder as she passed. "Bear it alone. I love him, come what may."

The door caught when she closed it, and I wept.

※ ※ ※

"We can't celebrate it, but it's good news all the same," Mrs. Stewart said over supper. She doled out slices of pigeon pie with a fierce efficiency, quick to take up her own silverware as if urging us to hurry. "Mrs. Holbrook will come to understand that."

"Have you asked Dr. Rea?" Zora held her knife and fork, a motion at eating a dinner she didn't intend to touch. Drawn and shadowed, she'd had little but tea and toast for days.

"That's why it's leftovers," Mrs. Stewart said. "He'll be waiting for us at six o'clock."

Cutting tiny bites of my pie, I wondered if there might be any way I could escape this. Though I wanted very much to be a party to Thomas' release from jail, driving the victoria straight into sunset terrified me.

Since Sarah's funeral, I strayed from windows at the first set of light; I busied my hands with mending the last pieces that needed packing before my departure that week-end. Prophecy did none a service, and I refused its practice. Like an open wound on my thigh, I carried Thomas' card with me always, a reminder of what would come. A reminder that my portents blew nothing but ill.

"They're a good sort, those detectives." Mr. Stewart broke a bit of crust with his fingers, a failure of courtesy he never would have made if we had no appointment to meet before us. "Said they shouldn't have arrested the boy at all. Had Emily listened to them that morning . . ."

Humming, Mrs. Stewart finished her lemon water, then sat back. "Mr. Pemberton and Mr. Bayles were quite plain about it. Badly written instructions or no, you cannot mistake an entire bottle for two tablespoons."

Chair legs squealed against the floor, and Zora took to her feet. She more than any was torn in this but put her napkin aside and summoned her grace. "I should like to change before we go. Excuse me."

"Zora," Mrs. Stewart called, abandoning her seat to follow.

Left alone with Mr. Stewart, I fished desperately for something to say. "Do you think I should stay behind to close the house?"

"I think offering your friendship to young Mr. Rea would be more useful." His gentle voice rolled with the words, and I was struck again at how very between them Zora was, half spitfire, half teasing elegance. Did he see it, I wondered, when he looked at her? Had Mrs. Holbrook seen resemblances when gazing on Sarah?

But I accepted his answer as counsel, and that's how I came to sit in the fore seat of the victoria with my eyes clamped shut. Like Nathaniel's gaze on me, I felt the sun slipping down to dusk. It came like a warm rain, cascading over me and dripping off as the moments passed. When the last glimmer of it drained away, only then did I look about.

"Thomas," Zora cried, and nearly jumped from the carriage before it stopped.

She took neither hand nor consideration of the public street when she threw herself into his arms. And dash propriety, he folded around her. Pressing his temple to hers, he swept her up, at last turning to mouth a kiss against her cheek.

They fit so exactly that none protested, and, indeed, the parents three kept apace for a moment to give them their reunion. They fit so exactly that none at all seemed troubled when Thomas said to her, as we drove back toward Reservoir Hill, "When we are married, I think we should consider Annapolis for ourselves."

"Close enough to visit," Zora said, without finishing the refrain that it was far enough away, as well. Gossip, unless very rich in blood, tended to dissipate on the road.

The drone of the horses' hooves lulled as darkness descended. It was not so very far from the station house to Division Street, and evening came on a pleasant breeze. It seemed a good number of lights brightened when we parked in front of the Reas' door, but people were good enough to espy us from indoors instead of out.

Caught in the moment, I spilled onto the walk before them, swirling out of their path as I asked, "You'll invite me, won't you?"

"Shhh," Zora said, shaking her head. "We can't even think of it until mourning's done."

She was right, of course. And reminded me still of the future in my pocket. That coming *September* bore into me — which September? It could be ten yet, or twenty—it could be the last ashen September of their old age together.

It drove me to distraction, caught like a bone in my throat. I thought on it a moment. Mayhaps Zora chose ignorance, and I wouldn't be the one to sway her. But maybe Thomas would not. I clasped my hands together, then offered them to Thomas once Mrs. Stewart set him free.

Leaning in, as if to murmur congratulations to him, I said, "Quick, would you know your future?"

But nothing came quick to Thomas. He lifted his head and made the most curious face. It spoke of nothing, save realization.

"Down, Amelia," he said.

And the best gentlemen of all of them put his hands on me. Called me by my given name! He grabbed me—right on the street, before Zora and her parents, and I wanted to protest!

An explosion came greater than thunder. Strange, astringent fire reflected in Thomas' eyes. In my confusion, I was mortified. Why would Thomas do such a thing? Why would he fall on me like a beast, and . . .

Then, slowly, I realized. I lay beneath him on the walk while his light and his breath drained out. I felt death weigh him, making him stone across my breast. His blood didn't splash on me — it seeped into me, through my gown, into my skin, until it stained me irrevocably.

And worst of all, the thing that echoed on was not the shot nor the silver peal of Zora's screaming. It was the words I heard in that last moment before the fire. A cold voice that I finally understood.

"Are you laughing now, Amelia?"

※ ※ ※

"We're searching for him," one man said.

"It's going to take some time yet, I'm afraid," another said.

Arms slung around myself, I stood on the back porch and stared numbly into the dark. I had met Thomas first through peeks at this yard. There was his line for laundry; there, his block for chopping wood. There, all still there, and he would never come back to it.

Somewhere, in the rooms behind me, Zora slept under the heavy, soothing hand of laudanum, and in the doctor's own theatre, the police stared at Thomas Rea's body, stripped to the waist.

How indecent it was to bare him like that for witnesses. How embarrassed Thomas would have been, to be seen so out of sorts and improperly dressed.

Something mechanical and awful twisted in me. It dared me to cry, and savagely refused to let me. Once again, I'd made my own fortune come true—and this time, so much worse than stealing a glove.

If I had held my guilt! If I had held my tongue! If I had done the right thing and burned all those cards . . . If Caleb's shot had been true—

How I wished it, how hysterically I wished that if Caleb had learned anything from Sarah, it would have been her good aim. Then I would be the one lying dead, just as he intended. I alone would be the last to suffer my poisonous visions.

Amelia, the wind murmured, and I, shameless, awful monster, walked into the night to meet it.

Nathaniel stepped from the shadows, his hands on me, bare and hot. They framed my face, the curve of my throat. He opened my wrap to stare at the wide stain that stole the sheen from mourning satin.

I had, I was certain, splashes of it on my skin. The police said I couldn't wash it off yet. And I was sure that even if I used steel wool and lye to scrub, that blood would mark me 'til my last.

"You should not have come."

"Where else would I be?" He jumped to the top step, looking indoors at the mass of gawkers that stomped through Dr. Rea's row house. None noticed that the back door stood open. Not one eye turned toward the two of us standing in shadows in the yard.

Made certain of that, Nathaniel came down again and caught my arms, pulling me toward seclusion. "Come away, Amelia."

"I can't."

Nathaniel frowned. "Why not?"

A hook pulled viciously through my numbness, a red hot wound through my chest that put me close to tears again. "I can't leave Zora alone! I can't leave at all. Nathaniel, I've killed someone tonight."

"Did you?" Nathaniel stepped closer, his voice urgent. "Did you fire the gun?"

I wanted to slap or scream. Instead, I swayed toward his heat and murmured. "It was meant for me. It was mine; I should be the one lying in there. Would you want to draw me? Isn't that how you met Thomas, over an autopsy? If it were me . . ."

"Amelia, stop it."

I begged mercy with myself, when the spice of Nathaniel's

cologne mingled with Thomas' blood, and resisted. Pulling away from him, I whispered, "Go away. I've got to give my account."

Incredulous, Nathaniel caught my hand and pulled me near. "What difference will your accounting make? Does it bring Thomas back?"

"Don't handle me!" I cried, too loud.

With another jerk, I pulled away, insensible and dizzy, then threw myself against him. Pressing my ear to his chest, I listened to his heart beat when mine did not.

One wretched sob spilled out, murdered when I clapped my hand to my mouth. He murmured nothing sounds against my ear, binding me close in his arms, warm there, safe there, if only in that moment.

When I caught my breath again, I told him, "There are better things for you. I wish you'd go."

"I won't," he said. "You haunt me. You alone. You're my fire. I'm your air."

And there, longing for it, needing it, I rose up to kiss him. Because I refused to see, I didn't know what would come in the days soon to follow. I needed him, imprinted on my lips, and in my heart, to help me bear the awful possibilities.

Pressing my hands to his cheeks, I drew my touch down to memorize the shape of him, murmuring as I broke away. "Come for me if I call."

"As ever," he said.

With two fingers, I smeared my kiss across his lips, then my own. Turning away so I would not see him go, I marched toward the house and slipped inside, I thought at first unnoticed. But when I raised my head to steal a glance back, to see the yard empty, I tangled first in blue eyes.

Mattie clung to Mrs. Stewart's arm. And Mrs. Stewart cut through me with a steel gaze.

"Didn't I say he beguiled her?" Mattie asked, and she dared—she dared! To give *me* a look, equal measures pity and sympathy. "I had to tell her, Amelia. I couldn't let you be blamed. You've been under his hand since the Sons of Apollo—we both know it."

"What have you done?" I demanded, clutching at a world that started to slip away.

"I only tried to save you," she said.

Then for me, all went black.

To put me on the first boat back to Maine, Mrs. Stewart paid the difference in my ticket from her own pin money and hired a cab to take me immediately to the docks.

It was the only way she could be sure I wouldn't see Zora again. Zora, fragile and empty as an eggshell—she deserved better than me, everyone agreed. My games killed Thomas. Then I was caught kissing in the garden with his blood still on my skin.

I was the monster. They saw it very clearly. They hadn't even needed the sunset for it.

Before I boarded, I turned back to look at the city of my summer. All the huddled row houses clung together, making blocks of streets, and neighborhoods of blocks. Horse cars rang their merry bells, and Arabers called—*apples apples apples and an orange! oranges!* All the color of it seared on my skin, red brick, white marble, blue skies.

Though I felt water beneath my feet, breathing in nothing but the fish and salt flavor of it from the docks, I called to Nathaniel all the same. I stood there long minutes, 'til at last the porter touched my shoulder and bade me board straightaway.

Nathaniel didn't answer—not on the waves nor the rocky shore of Maine, where I came in after dark. Neither brother nor sister-in-law had come to claim me—they hadn't even sent a dowager to be my chaperone on the long road from Portland to Broken Tooth.

As the driver packed my trunk away, I stood on solid earth and begged, with voice and all, to the wind. "Please, Nathaniel, please."

I even, in all madness, took his glove from my pocket and rubbed it against my face as I called. It smelled still of him, of bay rum, of the Maryland winds that had once carried us both.

Unimpressed by my madness, the driver stalked round to open the rockaway's door for me. For having seen one so close, so recently, I cared not to climb into this hearse; I didn't wish to let it carry me to my tomb on the rock. A prickling breeze came off the water, and I spun toward it.

"Please," I begged, tears starting to fall when I saw naught but the desolate pier behind me.

Clearing his throat, the driver said, "If you're waiting for Witherspoon, miss, your brother gave me a message."

I forgot myself. I clutched his lapels. I begged, "What is it?"

"It came down on the wire," the driver said. He unfolded a scrap produced from his jacket pocket and read it bloodlessly. "Fire in Mount Vernon Place. Stop. Mr. C. Grey arrested. Stop."

Struggling to keep my feet beneath me, I snatched the telegram and read the last line on my own.

WITHERSPOON DEAD.

❄

Oakhaven

Broken Tooth, Maine

Autumn 1889

❄

Nineteen

IN SPITE OF the cold sweeping between branches and across our precarious cliff, Lizzy scrubbed at shirts on the back porch. In spite of the cold that had filled up my heart, I let myself onto the porch and forced myself to meet Lizzy's eyes.

"I could do that," I offered.

"Thank you, no." She shook her head, a curl escaping to bob against her brow. Her raw hands clutched the scrub brush. Steam drifted from the tub, water boiled on the stove that she'd carried out—cleft to her schedule as she always had been.

Before I went to Baltimore, I'd found her precision

disconcerting. Each day was a day for something: Monday mending, Tuesday sewing, Wednesday washing.

How endlessly she toiled; how endlessly she taught me to do the same. She was sentenced to drudgery under my idiot brother's watch and cursed to raise his feral, backwoods sister into some good sort of woman.

I'd had no sympathy before. How viciously innocent I was, to think there was nothing more to Lizzy than ironing on Thursday and canning on Friday. There, watching her shiver and scrub, her head full of ugly words I'd put there — I had a realization.

It was no vision, no sending from another time or another place. The elements came into it not at all. It was simply my own head, and my own new shame, reminding me that what destruction I brought on myself and all those around me had no need to continue. I could end myself or go forward, and that was the truth of it.

Rubbing my throat to warm it, I coaxed my voice out again. "I wish I could undo it, Lizzy."

She scrubbed a moment more, then stopped. Resting her arms on the top of the washboard, she turned her slow gaze on me. "Which part?"

Caught short, I considered a moment. "Everything that embarrassed you. Or hurt you. Only some of the things troubling August. For a man of leisure, he's entirely too tense." My brief flare of humor guttered out as I went on. "Every disaster I visited on Zora."

Her expression turned keen. "And that's all?"

Closing my mouth, I stood there; I dug into the remains of my summer in Baltimore. And though I could list a hundred petty shames and failures, I had already named to her the ones I truly regretted.

I no longer cared that I couldn't be a good, quiet girl, satisfied with a comfortable life and a pleasant-enough husband. It hardly mattered that I was ruined and alone. For one sunlit season, I had laughed and I had loved and I had been extraordinary. It was a glorious ruination—my madness was mine—and for that, I was *not* sorry.

Pulling my shoulders back, I nodded. "That's all."

"I see," Lizzy said. She returned to her wash, brushing damp curls from her cheek before starting to scrub again. She didn't look at me again. But as she ground lye soap into paste, she did warn me, "The sun's setting. You should hurry inside now."

Out of penance or piety, I did as she said.

When I woke to my name, it was no mystery who spoke it. Lizzy stood over me, lit by the stub of a candle she'd fixed in a teacup. The thick weight of her hair coiled over her shoulder in a braid, and she clutched at the front of her dressing gown. "Are you awake?"

I nodded, though I hadn't quite left all haze of sleep behind. "What's the matter?"

With a gentle firmness, Lizzy pulled me to sit, then turned away. Leaving the candle on my bedside table, she swept through the dark to pick up a bundle that she had left on the foot of the bed. "Get up."

Like a clockwork machine, I found my feet and stepped into the silver pool made by moonlight through my window.

"Out of that gown," Lizzy said, as if I were a child. She even came over to help, tossing froth and lace into a bed still warm with the impression of my body. "Here, these should fit."

She pressed a muslin shirt into my hands, then a wool coat and pants. I frowned at their cut, raising my head to peer at her. Had she taken leave of herself? Had my prediction plunged her into insanity? They had me, so it wouldn't have surprised me in the least.

"Aren't these August's?"

"Mmm," she agreed, pulling a key from her pocket to unlock my trunk. "Dress, Amelia. I don't want to ask you again."

I found it obscene, how quickly I could put on a man's clothes. A few buttons, a few hooks, and nothing clasping me beneath all those layers but a loose night corset.

When I came around the bed, I nearly fell over my own feet. I knew best how to walk against the weight of bustles and petticoats, skirts and overskirts, polonaise aprons and wrappers—my legs felt entirely unclad and too unencumbered to bear.

"Shoes," she said, pushing a pair toward me as she retrieved the pack again.

"Lizzy," I said, a wavering spark of humanity lighting in my chest. She'd petted me, comforted me, and I had given her none but grief in return. She hadn't let me apologize before—though, to be fair, I hadn't tried. I'd only wished to undo things. I hadn't been brave enough to kneel before her and beg forgiveness. "About the things I wrote . . ."

Shushing me, Lizzy reached back for my hand and led me to the stairs. Quick down them—she so light on her feet, it reminded me of Zora—we came to the front door quick apace, and then she slipped the satchel from her arm to mine.

"There's fifty dollars tucked in the front," she said. She came across to me clear as water, not even unkind as she opened the door. "That should do for a train ticket or ship's passage, if you don't want to roam far."

I caught my laughter before it rose up, before it woke the house. "You're turning me out. Good girl, Lizzy."

With all her grace, Lizzy summoned herself, shorter by inches, but managing to stand taller all the same. Clasping my face between her hands, she made me look at her. She made me still and hear her, when she spoke, for her voice was gentle and made softer in deference to the night.

"I would never turn my sister out," she said.

I interrupted. "And yet?"

"I've been told all along that I could no more conceive than I could taste the cheese on the moon. You're selfish right now and cruel, but I'm not turning you out for my hurt feelings."

"Then what is this?"

Lizzy caressed my cheek, tracing the round of it with her thumb before stepping back inside. "If I can miscarry, I can conceive. That's hope."

"Lizzy . . ."

"For you, freedom. Be the woman you long to be, Amelia." She waved a hand at me, shooing me away as we might the hens from the back door. "I'll tell August I woke in the night to find you missing. He'll not come for you, I promise that. But you should go."

Plaintive, I clung to my place. I had no home anywhere, neither Maryland or Maine, not Kestrels, not Oakhaven. My parents were long dead; the Stewarts would never have me. August was the only family I had. Clinging bereft to the satchel she gave me, I asked, "But where?"

"That's the price of it. It's your future. Do what you like." With a smile and a shrug, Lizzy closed the door between us.

The heavy bolt turned, punctuating her point that I was free to go—anywhere but here. I almost preferred my coldness, my madness, and I wondered what would happen if I laid on the step and waited for morning.

Just then a wind came up. It kissed the back of my neck, cool and sweet with the scent of bay rum. Its fingers slipped into my collar, across my throat, tugging at the sunset charm. Consumed, I spun blindly and fell—into the black and gold glimmer of going on the wind, into strong arms.

"Could you have possibly put more water between us?" Nathaniel asked.

Everything moved within me, my rusted machinery grinding once more to life. I felt magic again; the air sparked with wonder. I could not take in enough of him, his round face and narrow eyes unmarred, his dark hair fallen in a careless wave across his brow. Nathaniel Witherspoon was whole and real and warm. And yet he'd seemed so many things in a vision, and wasn't madness a kind of vision?

To be certain of him, I murmured, "Aren't you dead? Wasn't there . . ."

"You're the only fire that consumes me." And my wonderful monster, he smiled at that. He smiled at me.

Clutching him, I buried my face against his shoulder. I had no more tears; no more hopes or expectations. I would outlive my great sin—and I would wonder another day if I could ever pay for it. But for that moment, I had no more fear.

Still buried in him, I asked, "If I told you to take me away?"

"I'd tell you to be more specific," he said. His fingers played against my spine, prodding me for the fire he knew lay within.

I wasn't ready to face Zora again—and she was all that remained of import in Baltimore. But she guided me yet and gave me a direction to take. I heard her voice, from our very first conversation—a prophecy of her own. Raising my gaze to his again, I said, "I order you to take me to Chicago. I hear the future's there."

In reply, he moved to kiss me, but I turned my face at the last moment. His breath skimmed hot against my cheek, and I whispered back against his. "No. First, tell me you love me, as you have no one else."

The wind roared around us, like a great storm come off the waves. Nathaniel tightened his arms around me and said, "Jump with me."

And I did.

Acknowledgments

My many, humbled, thanks to

Julie Tibbott, who asked amazing questions, excited me with her enthusiasm, and made this book more in every way.

Sara Crowe, for looking into the fires and believing in this book's future.

Jim McCarthy, for taking me on despite the fantastic mess I presented to him in the worst query letter ever.

Jay St. Charles from Pacific Yew Longbows, for helping me do even greater damage to Sarah Holbrook than I'd originally intended.

Carrie Ryan, for our red shoes and everything, everything else. I couldn't imagine trying to do this without you, and I'm so glad I'll never have to.

Aprilynne Pike, for dropping everything and reading an entire novel on her iPhone *at the gym* so I could have notes the same night—and for a thousand other amazing things. I promise to always get you to the airport on time.

Kami Garcia, for giving me homework and being the most incredible, enthusiastic literary ally in the history of books. Southern Gothic forever!

The Sarah Army: MacLean, Cross, and Rees Brennan for comfort, cosseting, and promises of assassination. Not to mention all the makings-out and other explosions, except in the way I just did mention them.

R. J. Anderson, the extraordinary and the classical, a most unexpected and entirely beloved ally. Dennis, can you hear me?

Jackson Pearce, for giving me a hard time (sorry, he's still dead, boo); *L. K. Madigan*, for all the outrage and cheerleading; *Megan Crewe*, for reading and book-twinning; and *Myra McEntire*, for a fast read, Binbons, and encouraging the dirty hot.

Cynthia Leitich Smith, for encouraging, mentoring, and inspiring always; and *Jeannine Garsee* and *February Grapemo*, where all the good things begin.

The Debs, each and every one, for being an absolute feast of awesome and the best writing group ever.

Wendi, for brainstorming, sceneforming, namestorming, babysharing, and everyday out-of-this-world, totally supernatural awesomeness. Thank you for being my muse. Thank you for being my one in five million. Thank you for everything.

Jason, for staying cool when I can't, for finding apostrophes I dropped, and for cheerfully saying yes every time I ask, "Could you read this?" Thank you for being my rock. Thank you for being my center. Thank you for everything.

DA DEC 07 2011